Stories of Ireland

BRIAN FRIEL

With an introduction by Louise Kennedy

PENGUIN BOOKS

PENGUIN BOOKS

UK | USA | Canada | Ireland | Australia
India | New Zealand | South Africa

Penguin Books is part of the Penguin Random House group of companies
whose addresses can be found at global.penguinrandomhouse.com.

Penguin Random House UK,
One Embassy Gardens, 8 Viaduct Gardens, London SW11 7BW

penguin.co.uk
global.penguinrandomhouse.com

Penguin
Random House
UK

First published as *Selected Stories* by The Gallery Press (ed. Peter Fallon) 1979
This edition published by Penguin Books 2025
002

Set in 11/13pt Bembo Book MT Pro
Typeset by Jouve (UK), Milton Keynes
Printed and bound in Great Britain by Clays Ltd, Elcograf S.p.A.

The authorized representative in the EEA is Penguin Random House Ireland,
Morrison Chambers, 32 Nassau Street, Dublin D02 YH68

A CIP catalogue record for this book is available from the British Library

ISBN: 978-1-405-97223-9

For Tom Kilroy

Contents

Introduction

I knew little, when I was asked to write this introduction, about Brian Friel's short stories. Though my brief is to offer a personal response, after reading I found myself wondering about their provenance, and Peter Fallon of Gallery Press, Friel's Irish publisher, was immeasurably generous in this regard. I was not surprised that the thirteen short stories that make up this collection are exceptionally good, but I was stunned to learn that nine of them originally appeared in the *New Yorker*. Excerpts from the correspondence between Friel and Roger Angell, his editor there, can be found in *Brian Friel: Beginnings* by American academic Kelly Matthews, from which a portrait emerges of a new writer, having given up his job as a maths teacher, balancing the demands of a rigorous mentorship with the material needs of his young family; his humility, his commitment to his art, his willingness to learn.

Friel selected these stories with the help of Seamus Deane, his friend and long-time collaborator at Field Day Theatre Company, and three more were later added by Friel's widow, Anne. Perhaps these are the ones Friel was most proud of, but there is a coherence – in place, in time and in theme – that makes me suspect they were chosen because they fit together. The world in which they play out is its own fictional universe, and there are even mentions of Ballybeg – derived from Baile Beag, the Irish for 'small town' – the fictional 'village of the mind' in which Friel set his plays. Indeed it is difficult to read *Stories of Ireland* without considering his later dramatic work, and there is much to think about. Throughout, the dialogue is so pitch-perfect and the characterization so unnervingly convincing – surely prerequisites for a playwright – that a four-way conversation flows without any need to state who is speaking. The seeds of his plays are here in more specific ways. In the mouldering, once beautiful 'Foundry House', we recognize the decaying pile in *Aristocrats*. In both 'The Diviner' and 'The Illusionists', a deadbeat chancer with a drinking problem and claims of special powers seems to be an early incarnation of both *Crystal and Fox* and Frank Hardy of *Faith Healer*. 'My Father and the Sergeant' offers a tentative examination of the duality that comes to powerful fruition in the public and private sides of Gar O'Donnell in *Philadelphia, Here I Come!* And how lovely to recognize the Donegal sisters of 'A Man's World' from *Dancing at Lughnasa*.

There is a border sensibility here, sometimes physically but more often psychologically, and a liminality: the sense of being between things. A village on the wrong side of a mountain, the side that gets little light; the British naval frogmen with their brusque efficiency coming over the border; a little boy speaking like the cowboys he's seen in films, unaware that by the end of the day he'll no longer be a child. The class and social strictures of Friel's world make for an uneasy order in which the doctor, the bank manager and the merchant, often with an elevated vantage, literally look down on everyone else; when these elements collide, uncomfortable truths surface. A sense throughout that the old world is meeting the new and they don't quite know what to make of each other.

A short story is a taut, delicate thing. Pull it too tightly and it will break up; not tightly enough and it will lack impact. There are all sorts of advice out there about its necessary components, most of which should be disregarded, but I do agree that by the end, something must have changed. Brian Friel's short stories, of course, deliver this. Sometimes the flashy appeal of magic or money momentarily turns a head, making the reality of its hollow charms all the more devastating.

Sometimes a character is forced to face the limits of their own agency, or reckon with the workings of their own black heart. Frank O'Connor named his working theory of the short story *The Lonely Voice*, a title that beautifully evokes the form's typical protagonist. But for Friel's characters there is often an intervention. A man tries to shield a widow from the shameful cause of her husband's death; an aging adventurer guards his young friends' futile dreams of finding sunken treasure; watching his son playing, a man comes to terms with the vagaries of his own memory. Often the interventions arrive too late, but that doesn't matter; what does is that someone tried, and it is in those white lies, the bumbling, mistimed attempts at connection, that this book's magic lies. And the prose is glorious.

Louise Kennedy

The Diviner

During twenty-five years of married life Nelly Devenny was ashamed to lift her head because of Tom's antics. He was seldom sober, never in a job for more than a few weeks at a time, and always fighting. When he fell off his bicycle one Saturday night and was killed by a passing motorcycle no one in the village of Drumeen was surprised that Nelly was not heartbroken. She took the death calmly and with quiet dignity and even shed a few tears when the coffin was lowered into the grave. After a suitable period of mourning she went out to work as a charwoman, and the five better-class families she asked for employment were blessed for their prompt charity, because Nelly was the perfect servant – silent, industrious, punctual, spotlessly clean. Later when others, hearing of her value, tried to engage her they discovered that her schedule was full; all her time was divided among the bank manager, the solicitor, the dentist, the doctor, and the prosperous McLaughlins of the Arcade.

Father Curran, the parish priest, was the only person she told she was getting married again, and he knew she told him only because she had to have a baptismal certificate and letters of freedom.

'He's not from around these parts, Nelly, is he?' the priest asked.

'He's not, Father.'

'Is he from County Donegal at all?'

'He's from the West, Father,' said Nelly, smoothing down the hem of her skirt. 'Of course, Mr Doherty's retired now. He's not a young man, but he's very fresh-looking.'

'Retired?' the priest said promptingly.

'Yes, Father,' said Nelly. 'Mr Doherty's retired.'

'And you'll live here in Drumeen with – with Mr Doherty?'

'That is our intention, Father.'

'Well, I wish you every blessing, Nelly,' said Father Curran in dismissal, because he was an inquisitive man and Nelly was giving nothing away. 'I'll see you when you get back.' Then quickly – an old trick of his – 'The wedding is in the West, did you say?'

'That has to be settled yet, Father,' said Nelly calmly. 'It will just be a quiet affair. At our time of day, Father, we would prefer no fuss and no talk.'

He took the hint and let her go.

Nelly Devenny became Nelly Doherty and she and her husband moved into her cottage at the outskirts of the village. Drumeen's speculation on Mr Doherty was wild and futile. What age was he? Was he younger than Nelly? What part of the West did he come from? What had he been – a train driver, a skipper of a fishing boat, a manager of a grocery shop, a plumber, a carpenter? Had he any relatives? Had he even a Christian name? Where had they met? Was it true that she had put an advertisement in the paper and that his was the only answer? But Nelly parried all their probings and carefully sheltered Mr Doherty from their clever tongues. The grinding humiliation of having her private life made public every turn-about in bars and court-houses for twenty-five years had made her skilled in reticence and fanatically jealous of her dignity. He stayed in the house during the day while she worked and in the evening, if the weather was good, they could be seen going out along the Mill Road for a walk, Nelly dressed entirely in black and Mr Doherty in his gabardine raincoat, checked cap, and well-polished shoes, the essence of respectability. And in time the curiosity died and the only person to bring up the subject now and again was McElwee, the postman, who had been a drinking pal of Tom Devenny, her first husband. 'I'm damned if I can make head or tail of Doherty!' he would say to the others in McHugh's pub. 'A big, grown man with rough hands and dressed up in good clothes, and taking walks like that – it's not natural!' And McElwee was also puzzled because, he said, Mr Doherty had never received a letter, not even a postcard, since the day he arrived in Drumeen.

On the first Sunday in March, three months after their marriage, Mr Doherty was drowned in the bog-black water of Lough Keeragh. Several of the mountainy Meenalaragan people who passed the lake on their way to last Mass in the village saw him fishing from Dr Boyle's new punt, and on their way home from the chapel they found the boat, waterlogged, swaying on its keel in the shallow water along the south shore. In it were Mr Doherty's fishing bag, his checked cap, and one trout.

Father Curran went to Nelly's house and broke the news to her. When he told her she hesitated, her face a deep red, and then said, 'As true as God, Father, he was out at first Mass with me,' as if he had accused her of having a husband who skipped Mass for a morning's fishing. (When he thought about her strange reaction later that day he concluded that Mr Doherty most likely had not been out at first Mass.) He took her in his car out to the lake and parked it at right angles to the shore, and there she sat in the front seat right through that afternoon and evening and night, never once moving, as she watched the search for her husband. When Father Curran had to go back to Drumeen for the seven o'clock Devotions – in an empty chapel, as it turned out, because by then the whole of the village was at Lough Keeragh – he had not the heart to ask her to get out. So he borrowed the curate's car and the curate took the parish priest's place beside Nelly. Every hour or so they said a rosary together, and between prayers Nelly watched quietly and patiently and responded respectfully to the curate's ponderous consolings.

Everyone toiled unsparingly, not only the people to whose

houses she went charring every day – her clients, as she called them: Dr Boyle; Mr Mannion, of the bank; Mr Groome, the solicitor; Dr Timmons, the dentist; the McLaughlins – but the ordinary villagers, people of her own sort, although many of them were only names to her. Logan, the fish merchant, sent his lorry to the far end of Donegal to bring back boats for the job of dragging the lake; O'Hara, the taximan, sent his two cars to Derry to fetch the frogmen from the British Admiralty base there; and Joe Morris, the bus conductor, drove to Killybegs for herring nets.

The women worked as generously as the men. They condoled with Nelly first, each going to where she sat in the parish priest's car and saying how deeply sorry she was about the great and tragic loss. To each of them Nelly gave her red, washerwoman's hand, said a few suitable words of thanks, and even had the presence of mind to inquire about a sick child or a son in America or a cow that was due to calve. Then the women set up a canteen in Dr Boyle's boathouse and made tea and snacks for the workers on the lake. Among themselves they marvelled at Nelly's calm, at her dignified resignation.

'The poor soul! As if one tragedy wasn't enough.'

'Just when she was beginning to enjoy life, too.'

'And they were so attached to each other, so complete in themselves.'

'Have his people been notified?'

'Someone mentioned that to Nelly, but she said his people are all dead or in England.'

'He must have got a heart attack, the poor man.'

'Maybe that . . .'

'Why? What did you hear?'

'Nothing, nothing . . . Nobody knows for certain but himself and his Maker.'

'Is it true that he took the doctor's boat without permission? That he broke the chain with a stone?'

'Sure, if he had gone to the doctor straight and asked him, he would have got the boat and welcome.'

'Poor Nelly!'

'Poor Nelly, indeed. But isn't it people like her that always get the sorest knocks?'

It was late afternoon before the search was properly organized. The mile-long lake was divided into three strips which were separated by marker buoys. Each strip was dragged by a seine net stretched between two yawls. The work was slow and frustrating, the men unskilled in the job. Ropes were stretched too taut and snapped. The outboard motors got fouled in the weeds. Then dusk fell and imperceptibly thickened into darkness and every available vehicle from Drumeen was lined up along the shore and its headlights beamed across the water. Submerged tar barrels were brought to the surface, the hulk of an old boat, the carcass of a sheep, a plough, and a cartwheel, but there was no trace of Mr Doherty. At intervals of half-an-hour a man in shirt and trousers went to the parish priest's car to report progress to Nelly.

'Thank you,' she said each time. 'Thank you all. You are all so kind.'

And immediately the priest beside her would resume prayers because he imagined that sooner or later she would break down.

Father Curran had just returned from Devotions and released the curate when the two frogmen arrived. They were English, dispassionate, businesslike, and brought with them all the complicated apparatus of their trade. Their efficiency gave the searchers new hope. They began at the north end, one taking the east side, the other the west. Carrying big searchlights they went down six times in all and then told Dr Boyle and Mr Mannion that it was futile making any further attempts. The bottom of the lake, they explained, had once been a turf bog; the floor was even for perhaps ten yards and then dropped suddenly to an incalculable depth. If the body were lying on one of these shelves they might have found it, but the chances were that it had dropped into one of the chasms where it could never be found. In the circumstances they saw no point in diving again. They warmed themselves at the canteen fire, loaded their gear into O'Hara's taxis, and departed.

The searchers gathered behind the parish priest's car and discussed the situation. Nelly's clients, the executives, who had directed operations up to this point, now listened to the suggestions of the workers. Some proposed calling the search off until daylight; some proposed pouring petrol on portions of the lake and igniting it to give them light; some proposed calling on all the fire brigades in the county and having the lake drained. And while the Drumeen people were conferring, the mountainy Meenalaragan men, who had raised the alarm in the first place and had stood silent, watching, beside the drowned man's waterlogged boat throughout the whole day as if somehow it would divulge its secret, now bailed out the water and, armed with long poles, searched the whole southern end of the lake. When they had no success they returned the boat and slipped off home in the darkness.

The diviner was McElwee's idea. The postman admitted that he knew little about him except that he lived somewhere in the north of County Mayo, that he was infallible with water, and that his supporters claimed that he could find anything provided he got the 'smell of the truth in it'.

'We're concerned with a man, not a spring,' said Dr Boyle testily. 'A Mr Doherty, who lies somewhere in that lake there. And the question is, should we carry on with the nets or should we wait until the morning and decide what to do then?'

'He'll come if we go for him,' McElwee persisted. 'They say he's like a priest – he can never refuse a call. But whether he takes the job on when he gets here – well, that depends on whether he gets the smell of the –'

'I suggest we drag the south end again,' said Groome, the

solicitor. 'The boat was waterlogged when it was found; therefore it can't have drifted far after the accident. If he's anywhere that's where he'll be.'

'We'll wait until the morning,' said McLaughlin of the Arcade. 'There's no great urgency, is there? Wait until we have proper light.'

'I vote for getting the diviner,' said McElwee. 'He likes to work while the scent is hot.'

'It's worth trying,' said one of Logan's men. 'Anyhow, what are you going to do tomorrow – try the nets again? After what the frogmen told you?'

Most of the men agreed.

'All right! All right!' said Dr Boyle. 'We'll get this fellow, whoever he is. But we'll tell Father Curran first.' They went round to the front of the car and the doctor spoke in to the priest.

'It has been suggested, Father,' he said, choosing his words as carefully as if he were giving evidence at an inquest, 'that we send for a diviner in County Mayo, a man who claims to be able to – to locate –'

'A what?' the priest demanded.

'A diviner, Father. A water diviner.'

'What about him?'

'It appears, Father, according to McElwee and some of the men here – it appears that this diviner has been successful on occasion in the past. We are thinking of sending for him.'

Father Curran turned to Nelly.

'They're going to send for a water diviner now,' he said, putting a little extra emphasis on the word 'now'.

'Whatever you say, Father,' said Nelly. 'I'll never be able to repay you for all your kindness this night.'

'Well, Father?' said the doctor.

'It's up to yourselves,' said the priest. Then, in dismissal, 'Let us begin another rosary. "I believe in God the Father Almighty, creator of Heaven and earth . . ." '

McElwee and one of McLaughlin's apprentices set off after midnight for County Mayo. None of Nelly's clients offered a car so they travelled in a fifteen-year-old van belonging to McElwee's brother-in-law. After they left the searchers broke up into small groups, sat in the cars and lorries and tractors lined along the shore, turned off the headlights, and waited. The night was thick and breathless. The men talked of the accident and of Mr Doherty. Each group knew something more about the man than had been known previously. In one car it was known that his name was Arthur. Two lorries away it was decided that Mr Doherty was not as retiring as one might have thought; one night a boisterous bass voice was heard coming through Nelly's kitchen window. In the Arcade delivery van someone said that Dr Boyle was seen going into the cottage at least once a fortnight and Nelly was never known to be sick. In one of the tractors Nelly's frequent visits to the chemist were commented on. But these scraps of knowledge meant nothing; they were the kind of vague tales that might attach themselves to any stranger with a taste for privacy. The man at the bottom of the lake was still that respectable stranger in the good raincoat and the well-polished shoes.

The night was at its blackest when the pale lights of the returning van came bobbing over the patchy road. Immediately fifty headlamps shot across the water and picked out tapering paths on the gleaming surface. Car doors slammed and the lakeside hummed with subdued excitement. Father Curran had been dozing. He opened his eyes and smacked his lips a dozen times. 'What? What is it?' he asked.

'They're back,' said Nelly, sitting forward in her seat. 'And they have him with them.'

The diviner was a tall man, inclined to flesh, and dressed in the same deep black as Nelly and the priest. He wore a black, greasy homburg, tilted the least fraction to the side, and carried a flat package, wrapped in newspaper, under his arm. The first impression was, What a fine man!, but when he stepped directly in front of the headlights of one car there were signs of wear – faded, too active eyes, fingernails stained with nicotine, the trousers not a match for the jacket, the shoes cracking across the toecap, cheeks lined by the ready smile. He spoke with the attractive, lilting accent of the west coast.

McElwee and McLaughlin's apprentice, fluttering about the diviner like nervous acolytes, led him to Father Curran's car. He opened the door, removed his hat, and bowed to Nelly and the priest. His hair was carefully stretched across a bald patch. 'I am the diviner,' he said with coy simplicity.

Father Curran leaned across Nelly to get a closer look at him.

'What's your name? Who's your parish priest?'

He ignored the questions and addressed himself to Nelly. 'I will need something belonging to your husband, something that was close to his person – a tie, a handkerchief, a –'

'Will this do?' asked McElwee, thrusting the checked cap over the man's shoulder into the car.

'Yes, that will do,' the diviner said. 'Thank you.' Then, to Nelly, 'His name was Arthur Doherty.'

'Arthur Doherty,' Nelly repeated, almost in a whisper.

'And he was born and reared in the townland of Drung, thirteen miles north of Athenry.'

'Drung,' said Nelly. She licked her lips. 'Did you know him?'

'I travel the country and I meet many people. I will search for the stonemason, but I will promise nothing.'

'How did you know he was a stonemason? You must have known him.'

'In a manner of speaking. Just as I recognize you,' he said.

She leaned away from him. 'You don't know me! I never saw you before!'

'You are Nelly Devenny, a highly respectable and respected woman. You work for the best people in Drumeen.'

'That dirty toper McElwee,' McLaughlin of the Arcade broke in.

'I will do my best,' the diviner said, withdrawing from the car and smiling at her – a sly, knowing smile, a sort of wink without an eye being closed.

'Father –' Nelly began. She clutched the priest's elbow, her face working with agitation.

Father Curran did not heed her; he was sniffing the air. 'Whiskey!' he announced. 'That man reeks of whiskey!'

'Father, what will he do? D'you think he's going to do anything, Father?'

'A fake! A quack! A charlatan! Get a grip on yourself, woman! We'll say another rosary and then I'll leave you home. They're wasting their time with that – that pretender!' And he blessed himself extravagantly.

Neither Dr Boyle nor Mr Groome nor Dr Timmons nor Mr Mannion nor McLaughlin of the Arcade volunteered to take the diviner out. McElwee and he went alone, the postman at the oars, the diviner sitting on the bench across the stern. The checked cap lay on his knees. He had removed the newspaper wrapping from his package, revealing a Y-shaped twig, and now he held it carelessly in his hands by the forked portion, the tail of the Y pointing away from him. The others gathered along the shore in the gloomy corridors between the headlights and watched them pull out. Before the boat was ten yards away from the edge of the water Nelly left the priest's car for the first time that day and ran to join the watchers. The women gathered protectively around her.

The boat moved evenly up the lake. One minute it was part of the blackness, the next it was caught, exposed, frozen in a line of light projected by a headlight, then lost, then caught. Calmly, imperturbably, exasperatingly it went on revealing itself and losing itself, until the minutes of blackness seemed endless and the seconds of exposure mere flashes. But the pattern was regular – the vehicles were evenly spaced – and soon the eyes of the watchers knew to relax when the boat and blackness were one, but where it crossed a ribbon of light they devoured it, noted the new position of the oars, the slant of McElwee's back, the hunched, tensed shoulders of the diviner. No one spoke; no one dared speak. A word to a neighbour, a glance at one's watch, a look at Nelly's face and one might never find the punt again.

Then it disappeared. The watchers fastened on the next beam, waited, blinked, wondered had they missed it, stared again, murmured. Had it stopped? Where was it? Why the delay? Had it found something? Then it appeared again, moving slowly into the spotlight, first the bow, then McElwee, then the oars poised above the water, then the diviner, now standing rigid, his elbows bent, his hands at his chest, his head stiffly forward. There it sat, a yellow picture projected against the night. Seconds passed. A minute. Two minutes. Three minutes. To watch was pain. The picture dissolved, men and boat merging in a blur, then took shape again.

'Come out! Come out! Bring out the boat hooks!'

McElwee was on his feet, his face screaming into the light, his arms gesticulating wildly to an audience he could not see. 'He's here! Bring out the boats! He's here!'

No one stirred. Then, after a minute, a youth broke away from the crowd and leaped into a yawl, and another followed him, and then everyone was moving and calling for oars and lighting cigarettes and wading heedlessly out into the water. The women held Nelly's arms because she was trembling violently.

The body lay in twenty feet of water directly below the diviner's quivering twig. They brought it in to the shore and carried it up the gravel immediately in front of Father Curran's car. There they laid it on top of a brown sail.

McElwee got down on his knees beside the body. He closed

the eyes and the sagging mouth and knitted together the fingers of the rough hands. Then he adjusted the good gabardine rain-coat and the trousers and placed the two feet together.

'He was a good man,' said the priest. He was standing beside the car door close to the group of women that surrounded Nelly. He lifted his chin and allowed his eyelids to droop. 'He was a man who lived a quiet life and loved his God and his neighbours,' he said in his pulpit voice. 'At this moment he is enjoying his just reward. At the hour of his demise he was carrying his rosary beads – am I correct, McElwee?'

'I'll see, Father,' said McElwee.

He knelt again. While he worked the men and women in the circle around the body looked away, gravely studying each other or staring off into the darkness beyond the cars. Then McElwee rose to his feet and moved quickly out of the circle, holding the dead man's belongings against his chest, his shoulders rounded as if to protect them. 'I – I – we'll have to look again, Father,' he said, facing away from the car. He took off his jacket and placed it on the ground and laid several objects on it. Then he folded the jacket around them.

'Did you find the beads?' the priest said.

'The clothes are soaking wet, Father. It's hard to get your hand into the pockets.'

'What do you have there?'

The postman straightened up and turned towards the light. 'There are these,' he said, holding something in his wet hands.

'Is that his wallet?'

'Yes. And the watch.'

'Give them to me.'

Someone handed the wallet and the watch to the priest who gave them at once to Nelly.

'What else is there?' the priest asked.

'Nothing, Father.'

'There is something else in your jacket there, McElwee.'

'Show him, McElwee,' said the doctor quietly.

McElwee looked at his jacket on the ground. Then he opened it. There were two dark-green pint whiskey bottles lying on it, side by side. One of them had no cork; the other had been opened but the cork was still in it.

'Ho-ho, so that's it!' said Father Curran. 'And what are you doing with two bottles?'

'I found them,' said McElwee quietly.

'He found them!' the priest cried. 'And what –' He saw the faces in the circle and then realization hit him. He opened his mouth to speak again but closed it without a word.

Imperceptibly it was dawn, a new day vying with the priest's headlamps. No one spoke; no one moved. Then McElwee bent and folded his jacket over the bottles once more. He turned and glanced at the priest and then, in a voice that was no more than a whisper but which carried clearly above the lapping of the water and the first uncertain callings of the birds, he said, 'We'll say a rosary for the repose of the soul of Arthur Doherty, stone-mason, of Drung, in the County Galway.' He began the Creed and they all joined him.

While they prayed Nelly cried, helplessly, convulsively, her wailing rising above the drone of the prayers. Hers, they knew, were not only the tears for twenty-five years of humility and mortification but, more bitter still, tears for the past three months when appearances had almost won, when a foothold on respectability had almost been established.

Beyond the circle around the drowned man the diviner mopped the perspiration on his forehead and on the back of his neck with a soiled handkerchief. Then he sat on the fender of a car and waited for someone to remember to drive him back to County Mayo.

The Gold in the Sea

The *Regina Coeli* was the last boat to pull away from the harbour that evening. She was a twenty-footer of graceless proportions, without sails, and with two sets of oars. I would have preferred to go in one of the bigger boats, with engines and a full-time crew, but the hotel barman told me they did not welcome passengers.

'Con's your man,' he said. 'What he catches won't glut the market. But he has travelled a bit, and himself and Philly and Lispy are a comical trio. Aye,' he added, smiling at some memory, 'even if you don't catch much it's an education being out with Con.'

We were to have set out at eight, at the turn of the tide, but between one thing and another – each of the four of us stood a round of drinks, and then I called a fifth, because they had been so agreeable about taking me salmon fishing with them – it was almost nine before we climbed aboard. The July sun had withered and the Donegal hills were a sullen purple but the whiskey drew us together, making us feel intimate and purposeful.

'By God, sirs, you'll get more fish tonight than you ever dreamed of!' said Con. 'Nothing like a choppy sea to make them jump.' He reclined in the stern, an elbow on the tiller, bald and garrulous as Odysseus. He was quick with energy for all his seventy-two years. I sat in the bow facing him. Between us were Philly and Lispy, each taut on an oar. They were young men in their thirties.

We had become acquainted in the bar of the hotel where I was spending my two weeks' holiday. There had been no diffidence between myself and the locals because the appearance of the salmon in the bay two days previously created a happy urgency that made everyone in Ballybeg partners. After breakfast that morning I had watched the boats return from their first night out, gunwales low in the water, the fishermen ponderous and slow moving, as if they had risen, sated, from a huge meal. The tiny pier was crammed with vehicles – trucks, tractors, battered vans – and as soon as a catch was weighed and loaded on to a lorry the driver planted his elbow on the horn, stuck his head out of the window, and cleared a lane for himself with his oaths. The distraught official who supervised the noisy weighing had a moonface that was on the point of tears. 'Gentlemen, please!' he kept whimpering. Young boys on their way to school peered down into the half-deckers and saw five-, ten-, and twenty-pound salmon that would be ten-, twenty-, and forty-pound salmon when their friends from the far side of the mountain heard about them. The vehicles scraped one another. Tyres skidded on the wet, cobbled pier. Only the conquering fishermen were calm and aloof. In twos and threes they came up the steep road to the village with the walk of kings.

Philly was Con's nephew. They lived in different cottages on a jointly owned five-acre farm. Con was a bachelor ('But if I had a penny for every woman I handled, by God, sirs, I'd be a millionaire!') and his nephew, he told the bar with unnecessary gusto, was the father of seven daughters. 'But he'll sire a son yet, never worry!' Lispy, I learned, lived with two maiden aunts who doted on him, but not to the extent of allowing him to bring a bride into the house. He was a shy man whose quietness suggested depth and whose speech gave no explanation for his nickname. Perhaps he inherited it. When Lispy had gone to the toilet Con told me that Lispy got mad drunk once a year, on Saint Patrick's Day, when he chased the two screaming aunts out of the house and over the stunted fields. 'Just to assert his rights,' Con concluded. 'A saint when sober, but inclined to be sporty on that one occasion.' All three men were full-time farmers and part-time fishermen and by any standards they were very poor.

Two miles out from the harbour, free from the shelter of the headland, we were struck by a brisk Atlantic wind. We were now part of an impenetrable blackness.

'At this very moment, friend,' Con proclaimed, 'you're sitting on top of more gold than there is in the vaults of Fort Knox.'

'We'll get our share,' I said, thinking he was referring to the salmon which he had described earlier as being so plentiful that you could dance a reel on their backs and not wet a toe.

'Real gold!' he said. 'At this very spot, on an August morning in 1917, the *Bonipart* was sunk by a German submarine on her way from England to the USA. Fifty fathoms straight below us. A cargo of bullion.'

'*Boniface*', corrected Philly.

'There's no smoke without fire,' said Lispy. He had a weakness, I discovered, for proverbs that apparently had relevance only to private thoughts of his own.

'She was slipping down along the coast,' Con went on, 'when the Huns caught up with her here. By God, sirs, you've got to hand it to them Germans!'

'Was it never recovered?' I asked.

'*Boniface*', repeated Philly doggedly. 'He always gets the name wrong.'

'Two shells done it,' said Con. 'One in the bows that made her rise up like a stallion, and then one midships. She went down like a knife.'

'And you don't know for sure what she was carrying. No one knows that,' said Philly.

'Just two shells,' said Con. 'And – bang! – *requiescat* the *Bonipart*.'

'*Boniface*', said Philly, but without heart.

'Enough gold to develop all the underdeveloped countries of the world – including Alaska.'

'The last straw broke the camel's back,' said Lispy mildly.

'Right below our feet. By God, sirs, it's a wonderful thought, too, isn't it? It's there and it's safe and no one has laid a finger on it. Happy as an old lark.'

While the whiskey was still active in me I made a few confident calculations. Assuming we caught a hundred fish (this was modest; that morning the *St Brendan* had waddled into port with three hundred), averaging ten pounds per fish, our night's work, at the current wholesale price of eight shillings and six-pence per pound, would earn us four hundred and twenty-five pounds. I did the calculation again because this seemed a lot of money, but I got the same result. Then, as one does when easy wealth presents itself, I built myself a chalet above Ballybeg, bought a boat, hired a crew, set up a canning factory and an export business, and was getting down to the details of an advertising campaign when the ghostly hulk of a long power-boat suddenly rose out of the water beside me, towered over me for a second, and vanished, thrumming in the blackness. I was instantly cold and sober.

'By the look of them that was the McGurk brothers,' said Con casually. 'Damned near rammed us, didn't they?'

'Why haven't they a light?' I almost shouted.

'A light!' said Philly, with contempt. 'And have the patrol boat down on them for fishing without a licence? Are you mad?'

'Why don't they take out a licence?' I demanded.

'Costs money,' said Philly flatly.

'A stitch in time saves nine,' said Lispy.

'You mean to say,' I went on, 'that for all we know there may be dozens of boats all around us, not one with a light? And all of them poaching?'

'Not dozens,' said Philly. 'Maybe three or four.'

'And what happens if they get caught – if they don't drown us and themselves first?'

'Boat's confiscated. Gear's confiscated. Up to six months in jail.'

'Too good for them!' I shouted. 'It's a disgrace having –'

'By my reckoning, sirs,' Con broke in, 'we're near the Stags, and it's about time we shot the net. You can argue to your heart's content when we're drifting. Ship the oars, sirs, and let's get the net out.'

I heard him fasten the tiller with a rope and the handles of the oars spear towards me. I reached out to catch them and then it dawned on me for the first time that we had no light either.

I had examined the net earlier in the day. It was three miles long, four feet deep, made of nylon, and manufactured in Japan. It was designed to float about twelve inches below the surface. Con had explained that these Japanese nets were new to the Irish market and that they were so transparent the fish couldn't see them even in the daytime. I asked him if this meant that salmon fishing could now be done in the daytime, at which he laughed scornfully and replied that sure God and the world knew that you fished salmon only at night. I left it at that.

Now, while the boat drifted, the net was fed out from the stern. The job took the best part of an hour. The blackness was so dense that the three fishermen had identity only by their voices. Con, I gauged, was on the middle bench, issuing instructions, and Philly and Lispy were throwing out the net. They talked incessantly.

'Hurry up, sirs! It'll be dawn before you know.'

'Shut up!'

'The best salmon in the world are got in Peru.'

'How would you know?'

'I seen me in my day grilling a seventeen-pounder over an open fire near the town of Pisco, if you ever heard of it.'

'It's an ill wind that blows nobody good.'

'Come on, sirs! The seven daughters and the two aunts will think you've emigrated.'

'For a man with such a big mouth how is it you never got a thump across it during your famous travels?'

'We'll fill the boat tonight, sirs. I'll settle for nothing short of a boatload.'

'Look before you leap.'

'Gold, sirs. Cast out the net and bring in the gold.'

'Fit you better to talk less and work more.'

'This will be a lovely catch. And I've seen apples in Oregon that were as big as a bishop's head. And I seen oranges in San Paolo that two men, eating steady, couldn't get through in a week.'

'You and your stories. There's nothing as hateful as an old man that never stops talking.'

'Faraway hills look green.'

'This is the work'll put muscles on your backs, sirs. A season of this, Philly boy, and you'll father half-a-dozen sons.'

'A blathering old woman! Hateful!'

'There's no smoke without fire. Oh, God, no—no smoke at all.'

When the net was all out, its end was secured to the stern. Then the three men moved back to their first positions and the long, long wait began. For the next hour no one spoke, not even Con. Despite the sound of wind and sea and the rheumaticky groans of the *Regina Coeli* we seemed to be encased in silence. The elements made their blustering noises above and beyond, but in and around our floating arena there was a curious stillness. In the drifting blackness of the night I could hear Philly's deep, regular breathing and the coins rattle in Con's trousers every time he searched for matches to light his pipe. It was a strange sensation, floating in blackness across an unknown sea, with men one couldn't see but whose intimate movements one could hear distinctly. And as time crept by my senses sharpened and became responsive to a shift in the direction of the boat, to the slightest movement of a body, almost to the very presence of the fish beneath us. It was a strange, thrilling perceptivity, like playing blind-man's buff for the first time as a child. I wondered if the others experienced it, and as soon as this thought occurred to me I found myself going absolutely still, opening my mouth so that even my breathing would not be audible, speculating with absurd cunning that my thinking might be somehow perceptible.

Con's booming voice smashed the secrecy, and the noise of the wind and the seas crashed in.

'It was in the winter of 1918,' he said, 'and I was assing about in the region of a town called Fort Good Hope on the Mackenzie River, if you ever heard of it.'

'I did not,' said Philly curtly.

'And there was no work, and the whole damned place was under sixteen foot of snow, and there was a famine in my belly and not a cent in my pocket.'

'Oh-ho, oh-ho,' said Lispy mildly.

'So bloody bad was that winter, sirs, that the wolves came down from the hills, down into the very streets of Fort Good Hope, and ate all before them.'

'Pity they missed you – if you were there at all.'

'Anyhow, to cut a long story short, the townsfolk held a meeting, and it was agreed that they would pay a dollar out of the public funds for every wolf's head that was brought in to McFeterson's trading station. And a dollar in them days was something, sirs. You wouldn't light your pipe with a dollar in them days.' He waited for a comment. None came.

'So off I went into the hills with a Winchester –'

'Through sixteen foot of snow!' said Philly.

'– shot two dozen wolves, cut the heads off them, and carried them back to Good Hope.'

'Will you listen to the man!'

'Still waters run deep.'

'Presented my load to old Robbie McFeterson and said, "Twenty-four dollars, Robbie, please." Robbie counted the heads and gave me my money. And then says he, "Here, sonny boy, take them heads out the back and bury them." And that's what I done. Buried them in the snow behind the trading station, and then went back in and bought food and whiskey and had a hell of a week to myself. But when the week was up I was broke again and hungry again and my tongue was out a mile for a drink. So what did I do, friend?'

'You loaded the Winchester, Con,' I said.

'I went down that Sunday night to the plot behind the trading station and dug up them heads and the next morning presented them to Robbie! That's what I done! And he paid me – twenty-four dollars! And I done the same thing the following Monday and the following Monday and the following –'

'Damned things would have been rotten after four days!' Philly said.

'In twenty foot of snow, man? Fresh as a daisy! And old Robbie never suspected a thing. As straight a man as ever drew breath.'

'A man who never told a lie,' Philly said bitterly.

'By God, sirs, you've got to hand it to them Canadians!'

About two in the morning we had cold tea and huge hunks of homemade bread. The tea tasted of disinfectant and I furtively emptied mine over the side. I chewed mouthfuls of the bread until it became a thick, dry paste in my mouth, and then I tried to swallow it in a piece, without tasting it, the way one swallows medicine. When I had got through my ration Lispy insisted I share his – 'The old aunts aren't too bad at the soda bread' – and I took two more slices. One I ate with effort. The other I dropped into the sea and then wondered if it might not get caught in the net and be hauled back into the boat later.

After we had eaten Con resumed his tales of his travels;

Philly must have dozed because his uncle held forth without interruption. Lispy threw in an occasional proverb, perhaps to show that he was awake and listening. I was cold and tired and eager for the night to end. My dreams of a salmon industry had lost some of their sparkle.

It was still pitch black when they began to haul the net. It was then about 4 a.m. and the darkness was as dense as ever, but one felt it had lost its terrible permanence; a change was imminent. The blackness would soon be fragmented. When they began to haul the net – Philly and Lispy again doing the donkey work, Con instructing and encouraging, and me mumbling an occasional commendation just to establish my participation – we rediscovered the purpose and intimacy that had animated us when we had set out. We knew again that out of the black, invisible waters we were about to draw in a small fortune in fish. It was a lovely feeling.

'She's a grand boat, this,' Lispy said to me with sudden friendliness. 'And her name is *Regina Coeli*. That's Latin, and it means "Star of the Sea".'

They were still hauling when the sky and sea became distinct. The sky was a fuzz of mist that ringed our craft at a discreet distance. The last fifty yards of net had still to be pulled in when the sky suddenly broke into black and orange and grey streaks. I could see Con's bald head glistening with salt water and Philly's and Lispy's yellow waterproofs billowing like sails in the morning breeze. Now all the net was lifted. The young men straightened up and waited to get their breath back, and Con released the fish from the mesh. His broad shoulders concealed his movements. I could not see how many we had landed.

'Well?' said Philly.

'Salmon caught in the net, friend, is never as good to eat as salmon caught with a fishing line,' said Con. 'And I'll tell you why. When they get caught in the net they can't breathe, and

22

their lungs burst, and unless you gut them and pack them right off they go bad very quick.'

'How many's in it?' said Philly impatiently.

'But if you catch a fish with a rod and line,' Con went on, 'you kill him before his lungs burst and he's a better fish to eat – far better.'

'I asked you – how many are there?'

Con straightened and grimaced up at the sky. 'Six,' he said flatly. 'There's six in it. Six wee ones.'

'Oh-ho, oh-ho,' said Lispy.

Philly spat out a curse. There was a long silence.

'Right, sirs!' Con announced suddenly in a new, vigorous voice. 'Back to the oars, and home to the daughters and the aunts. There'll be another day. Oh, by God, there'll be another day!'

He moved back to the stern, and Philly and Lispy each took an oar, and we headed for home, taking our direction from a cold, grey sky. Six small fish, I calculated, would fetch about fifteen pounds – five pounds for each of the three men. Then I remembered Con telling me that the Japanese net cost eighty pounds, more than half of which had still to be paid. He said it could be lost in a storm or destroyed by seals before it had been paid off. To balance my rising sympathy I told myself that they were not, after all, real fishermen, but poachers; that they had no right to fish and so could not be disappointed with their catch. But it was no time for assessments. The sky had grown brilliant and the headland was strong and permanent ahead of us. The night was a failure. I was wet and hungry and miserable.

'At this very moment, friend,' Con proclaimed suddenly, 'you're sitting on top of more gold than there is in the vaults of Fort Knox.'

'You were telling me about that,' I said coldly.

'A cargo of bullion. Heading for the States.'

'Tell him about the salvage ship,' said Philly.

'None of us knows what it got – if it got anything,' replied Con sharply.

'Tell him all the same.'

'The proof of the pudding is in the eating,' said Lispy.

'What's this about a salvage ship?' I asked.

'Five years ago,' said Con, addressing me but watching Philly and Lispy with his sailor's eyes, 'on a clear spring morning, a Dutch salvage vessel dropped anchor at this very spot and didn't move away for twenty-seven days. She had divers and equipment and all the rest of it. But none of us knows did she get anything.'

'They weren't here for the good of their health,' said Philly. He turned to me. 'What do you think?'

'Take my word for it,' Con broke in. 'They got nothing. Didn't I watch them through the glasses day and night? And didn't I tell you dozens of times they pulled up nothing but seaweed?'

'You couldn't swear to it.'

'For God's sake, I'm not a swearing man. I'm telling you – the gold's still down there in the *Bonipart*.'

'*Boniface*'.

'Call it what you like. It's all there, happy as an old lark.'

'Maybe you're right,' said Philly, with surprising amiability. 'I'm not saying you're wrong. All I'm saying is that we don't know for sure.'

'Take my word for it,' said Con with finality. 'We're sitting on a gold mine.' He spoke with such authority that somehow we all felt that he must be right.

We were the first to tie up at the harbour. The place was deserted, silent in the clean morning light. There was only the sharp smell of old fish and the light, echoey sound of the water under the dock. Now that we were on land again our bodies were slow and unsure with fatigue. I thanked them for taking me with them and we shook hands formally. Con held me by the elbow until the young men were out of earshot.

'It wasn't much good, was it?' he asked.

'I enjoyed it, Con,' I said.

In the daylight he looked every one of his seventy-two years – an old man with tired eyes. 'The point is,' he said, 'the fish are there, a bloody harvest of them. You saw for yourself the catches them big boats landed. What we need is an outboard. That's what we need. I keep telling the boys that. "The fish is there," I say to them when they lose heart.'

He stood looking back at the sea, still holding my arm. Then he spoke in a rush. 'I told you a lie about the *Bonipart*.'

'Yes?' I said cautiously. I thought he was going to ask me for money.

'The Dutchmen cleaned her out from head to foot. I seen it all through the glasses from the point of the headland. They took cartloads of stuff off her. Didn't leave a bolt on her.'

'And was she really carrying bullion?'

He didn't hear me but went on as if I hadn't spoken.

'I don't want Philly or Lispy to know this. It's better for them to think it's still there. They're young men . . . You see, friend, they never got much out of life. Not like me.'

His voice trailed off and I suddenly understood that he was asking me for something more important than money.

'You saw the world, Con,' I said. 'You've been everywhere.'

'Damned right I have!' he said. 'Canada, the United States, South America – right round the world before I was twenty!'

He turned and we walked off the dock and started up the hill together.

'By God, sirs,' he said, 'you've got to hand it to them Dutchmen!'

The Widowhood System

The very day his mother was buried Harry Quinn set about converting the two attic rooms, from which she had ruled the house for the last nineteen years of her impossible dotage, into a model pigeon loft, so that he could transfer his precious racing birds from the cold, corrugated-iron structure in the back garden. The house, at 16 Distillery Lane, in chaotic condition, already consisted of Harry's ramshackle grocery shop on the ground floor and the flat of Handme Levy, a tailor, on the second. Handme – short for Hand Me Down the Moon (he was six-and-a-half feet tall if he was an inch) – helped with the task of reconstruction because midwinter was an even slacker time than usual in the tailoring business and because he was already in arrears to Harry, his landlord. Fusilier Lynch gave a hand, too, out of the goodness of his heart. For six days the three men worked, stopping only to eat the meals that Judith Costigan, who lived next door in Number 15, made for them. When the job was complete they carried the thirty-six pigeons in, two at a time, each man making six journeys out to the garden, in through the shop, past the smirking tailor's dummies in Handme's living room, and up to the top of the house. Then they drank in celebration. They drank, as they did after every race, win or lose, in the kitchen behind the shop.

'It's a powerful loft,' said Handme. 'Height and space and light.'

'A castle,' murmured the Fusilier.

'You waited one hell of a long time to get them inside, Harry,' said Handme. 'But it was worth waiting for.'

'A palace,' said the Fusilier.

Harry suffered from running eyes. They were never dry. Strangers who went into his shop were disturbed by the sight of the weeping shopkeeper. 'Now I'm going to tell you something, boys,' he announced, mopping his tears with a soiled handkerchief. 'Something that's been in my nose for nineteen years.'

'You're going to marry Judith!' said Handme.

'I'm going to produce the best racing pigeon Mullaghduff has ever seen. As a matter of fact, boys, I'm going to breed the first local pigeon ever to win the All-Ireland Open Championship.'

Handme's face was permanently fixed in the expression a man has immediately before he sneezes – mouth open, teeth bared, eyes wide, forehead wrinkled. On him it became a look of wild delight and anticipation. That, on top of a thin, gangling body, made the young girls of the town scared stiff of him. 'By God, Harry, you will, too!' he cried. 'Won't he, Fusilier?'

The Fusilier was short, stocky, silent. He was in his late forties, the youngest of the three bachelors. He was better at greyhounds and whippets than at birds, but a good all-rounder. 'How?' he asked cautiously.

'By science,' said Harry. 'I'll get my bird, train it the way you would train an athlete, feed it right, exercise it right, get to understand its psychology. It's a matter of science.'

'By God, you're right, Harry!' said Handme. 'The All-Ireland Open, no less! Eh?'

'And where do you propose getting this wonder bird in the first place?' asked the Fusilier.

Harry paused before he answered. 'I'm going to breed it,' he said.

'Huh!' The Fusilier laughed drily and began examining his corduroy riding breeches which were bald at the knees.

'I'm going to breed it scientifically,' Harry went on calmly, 'according to the theories, principles, and practice of Gregor Johann Mendel.'

'Is that the Galway buck that raced the wee grey hen last –?' Handme began.

'Gregor Johann Mendel says – and in case you boys never heard of him, he is a priest and a scientist – he says that a racing pigeon isn't a racing pigeon at all. A racing pigeon, he says, is a bundle of bloody genes. Get the right genes, says he, and you have the winner of the All-Ireland cooing in your lap.'

'What club is he in, this Mendel fella? Where's his loft?' the Fusilier asked.

'What I've been doing all my life, what every fancier in this country has been doing all their lives,' Harry went on softly, 'is mating the best cocks with the best hens. Quality with quality, stamina with stamina, speed with speed. And we've all been wasting our time.' He leaned across the kitchen table and wiped his eyes so as to get a moment's clear vision of his friends' faces. 'According to the Mendelian theory, when you breed champ with champ the offspring generally tends towards the average of the species, unless both members to the union are –' He faltered. The quotation he had learned from the *Pigeon Fanciers Post* began to fade. The word 'homozygous' pirouetted before his mind and vanished.

'Anyhow,' he went on, 'the point is this: quality with quality is no guarantee of quality young ones. Haven't we proved that ourselves? So what I'm going to do now, boys, is the very opposite: fast cock to slow hen, lazy cock to active hen. Until sooner or later I'll have a national winner in my loft. Trial and error – the scientific method. And, by God, boys, with the old woman out of the road and the place to myself there's nothing to stop me now!'

Later that night, when Harry invited his friends into Judith's house for supper, Handme told her of Harry's scheme. She laughed and said, 'Good for you, Harry!' and went on making them a huge feed of rashers and eggs. There never was a more even-tempered, more placid woman than Judith Costigan. When her young scut of a brother, Billy, whom she had reared, sailed for Canada one August morning, leaving her with no means of support except the knitting she did for the glove factory, she laughed and said, 'Aren't I lucky to have a roof over my head?' When old Mrs Quinn became bedridden and summoned Judith to feed and clean her Judith laughed and said, 'It's the least I could do for a neighbour.' And on those Saturday nights after a race had been lost or won, when Harry, Handme, and the Fusilier had drunk themselves silly and adjourned to Judith's to round the night off, she laughed most heartily because Harry invariably said to her, 'Judith Costigan, someday I'm going to ask you to marry me – someday when I'm good and sober.' It was a funny sight to see Harry swaying in the middle of the kitchen floor, his hand on his chest, his cheeks streaming with tears, and Judith, plump, smooth, hazel-eyed, fresher-looking than her forty-four years, nodding her head and laughing generously at him. It was so funny that Handme Levy would forget himself and begin to do a jig until his spinning head could no longer control his long, miserable shanks and he would fall into a chair and grimace wildly at the ceiling. Then the Fusilier would get maudlin about his time in the British Army – when, as he said, 'for four long years my stomach was starved for the whiff of a greyhound'. When they had sobered they would crawl home and they would not call on Judith again until the next race day, or until they wanted a well-cooked meal.

His mother was not dead a year when the laziest of Harry's hens, which he had paired with a cock with a broken wing, laid two white eggs. The awkward father knocked one of the eggs out of the nest and it smashed on the concrete floor. Out of the other egg came the bird that Harry was waiting for. Of course he did not know this until he saw it on the wing. But he knew then. Then there was no doubt at all. It was a small pigeon, blue-grey, with a white neck and a flat-topped head. Its great pectoral muscle filled its breast and stirred gently against the hand. Its back was broad and strong and straight.

Its legs were short. Its full, ovoid body was smothered in velvety feathers.

Handme examined it one Sunday morning. Then he passed it to the Fusilier. Harry waited for their comments. The lofts were open and the birds, in squadrons of fifteen, flew at the same height as the chapel bells, rolling over the tops of the pines and across the river and out over the barley fields and back to the peaks of the pines again.

'It's a good bird, all right,' said Handme. 'How does it take off?'

'Clean and straight,' said Harry.

'Any trouble in trapping it?'

'None. It lands on the platform and drops right down.'

'Aye, it's a good bird, all right,' said Handme. 'Isn't it, Fusilier?'

The Fusilier handed the bird back to Harry. 'It's a cock,' he said.

'It's what?' Handme squealed his surprise.

'I know it's a cock,' said Harry with dignity.

'But – but – Harry, you're not thinking of racing a cock, are you?' Handme spluttered. 'I mean to say, you never raced a cock in your life – it was always hens. The natural system – back to the nest –'

'And did I ever do anything worthwhile, racing the natural system?' snapped Harry, suddenly angry. 'Isn't that what all the fanciers round here are doing – racing the natural system? A flock of bloody turkeys waddling back to a cosy seat on eggs. And did any man of them ever win a national trophy in his natural life? Well, did they or did they not?'

'Not that I know of,' said Handme, subdued more by Harry's voice than by his argument.

'So,' said Harry quietly. 'I'm going to try the widowhood system. And I'm going to make a job of it.'

'You will, too,' said Handme. 'It's a grand bird, all right.'

'Have you mated him yet?' asked the Fusilier.

'Not yet,' said Harry. 'I'm going to mate him with a wee, fat red hen. I saw him eyeing her.'

'Is he keen?' said the Fusilier.

'How the hell would I know? He didn't confide in me!'

'There's nothing wrong with the widowhood system,' said the Fusilier calmly, looking out across the still, sabbatical town, 'only for the drawbacks. I seen cocks in my day that were so eager to get back to the hen they battered themselves against the basket and wore themselves out so that they were too tired to race. And I seen cocks in my day that didn't give a damn if they never saw the hen again. If you want a sure performance give me a hen every time. A hen will always hurry back to the nest. It's not called the natural system for nothing.'

'And what the hell do you think the widowhood system is?' said Harry, wiping his cheeks with the cuff of his jacket. 'What could be more natural than for a cock to fly back to its mate?'

'True for you, Harry,' Handme agreed, although he was thinking of the young girls of the town scattering in all directions when he met them coming out of the glove factory.

'Anyhow,' Harry went on, 'I'm sending him to Omagh next Friday week for a tryout the next day. You'll see then if I'm right.'

'Thirty miles is too far,' said the Fusilier. 'Send him to Omagh and that's the last you'll see of him.'

'Maybe the Fusilier's right,' said Handme. 'Why not try Strabane for a first outing? Fifteen miles is plenty for a first outing.'

'And you can't race him till he's mated first,' said the Fusilier.

'And you're not sure that the red hen'll have him,' said Handme.

Harry blinked his eyes and glared from one to the other. 'You two,' he said, his voice breaking with frustration, 'think you know everything! But you know damn all! This is my bird! And I'm going to race him from Omagh! And he'll mate for me! And he'll race for me – scientifically, by the widowhood system!'

He flung open the trapdoor and held the bird on the palms of his hands beneath it as if it were an offering. It spread its wings, hesitated a second, then rose up and out into the spring air where it joined a squadron of fifteen and tumbled in the waves of the singing bells.

Handme and the Fusilier were right; Omagh was too far. But in everything else they were wrong. On the Tuesday before the race Harry had paired the bird with the red hen, and she had acquiesced. And on the day before the race he had held the cock close to the hen until the cock's muscles tensed, but he had not allowed them to breed. Then he slipped the rubber race ring round the pigeon's leg, thrust the bird into the basket, and carried it down to the railway station. The know-all Fusilier was wrong in that detail, too; the bird did not batter itself against the sides of the cage. Indeed, Harry would have been happier if it had shown even some anxiety at being separated from its mate. But it was not an excitable bird, he consoled himself, and surely that was a good thing.

Four other pigeons from the local club were entered for that race and the best of them, Joe McSorley's checkered hen, clocked in seconds after 11.00 a.m. Major O'Donnell's two birds arrived next, at 11.15 a.m. and at 11.18 a.m. At 11.23 a.m. Harry saw Patsy Boyle's ten-year-old hen flit over the pine trees, as fresh as if she were starting out, and she had eight miles farther north to travel. This meant that her velocity was almost as good as the velocity of the Major's birds. Even though all the birds were released from the same place at the same time each had a different distance to travel back to its own loft and its speed over its own distance was what mattered. As soon as the birds were liberated each owner set his timing clock in motion and as soon as his bird returned he dropped its leg ring into the mechanism and thus stopped the clock. After the race these clocks were all submitted to the club for examination and the different times and distances were calculated and the winner determined.

The Angelus bell rang at noon. Harry went up to the loft for the eighth time. His cock had not returned. He boiled potatoes for his lunch and ate them. He washed the counter in the shop, mopped the floor, and disposed of flypapers that had been hanging from the ceiling since last summer. He climbed the stairs again. Still no bird. Then he threw a handful of maize inside the trapdoor, went down to Handme's bedroom and shook him awake. 'Keep an eye on the shop!' he shouted into the startled eyes. 'I'm away out for a pint.'

'The bird – is he back?'

'He'll come back in his own good time,' said Harry over his shoulder.

His own good time was at 6.30 that evening and by then Harry and Handme and the Fusilier were sozzled. It was the Fusilier who found him perched in the loft. The two others heard the Fusilier stumbling down the stairs singing to the bird, ' "You are my sunshine, my only sunshine. You make me happy when skies are grey." '

'Welcome back, wee cock!' cried Handme. 'Had you a nice holiday in New York?'

'Don't let me see him!' Harry called, crying into his hands. 'He disgusts me – that's what he does, disgusts me.'

'Shhh,' said the Fusilier. 'He's back, isn't he? Isn't that all that matters? Where's the clock? Gimme the timing clock and we'll drop his ring in – just for the record.' He kissed the bird gently on the back.

'Take him away!' Harry called. 'He disgusts me.'

'Hens every time,' said Handme. 'For reliability and dependability and –'

'Fling him in the loft out of my sight! I still have some bloody pride.'

'Now, now, now, boys,' said the Fusilier, holding the bird to his cheek.

'He went and had a holiday on top of the Statue of Liberty!' said Handme. 'That's what he done!'

'But he'll race!' said Harry. 'By God, he'll race before I'm done with him, or I'll know why!'

'He's nothing but a bundle of beans,' said Handme, believing he was quoting Gregor Johann Mendel.

'Yessir, he'll race! I'm not beaten yet, not by a long chalk!'

' "You are my sunshine, my only sunshine",' sang the Fusilier as he made his way up the stairs again.

That night ended in Judith's house. After she had fed them she saw Handme's dance and heard the Fusilier's reminiscences about army life and listened to Harry's tearful proposal. They did not leave her until almost three in the morning, and she was still laughing when she said goodnight to them.

In the following two months the bird was raced three times – from Monaghan; from Campbeltown, in Scotland; and from Wexford. Each time Harry set his timing clock but never submitted it to the local club for scrutiny after the bird had returned. When the other fanciers would ask him was he competing or was he not he would reply that he was entering but not competing. 'I just want him to get some practice,' he would say, 'but I don't want him to stretch himself until the All-Ireland.' And they would answer, 'Suit yourself, Harry. It's your bird,' and wink slyly at one another.

Handme came up with several explanations for the cock's indifferent performances. 'I've been studying its skull, Harry,' he said, the day after the Monaghan outing. 'That's where your troubles lie.'

'Aye?'

'It's my opinion, Harry, that the head isn't developed right, with the result that the brain is being squeezed in its cavity.'

'Is that your opinion?'

'Doesn't it sound sensible? I think that if we could get some way to develop its skull there wouldn't be that pressure on its brain. And if its brain wasn't being squeezed it could concentrate better on flying.'

'D'you know what I think, Handme?' Harry replied, with commendable control. 'I think that if you stuck to your sewing it might suit all of us a lot better.'

After the Campbeltown trial Handme's explanation was that the pigeon was allergic to salt water. 'It's my belief that he was going like a bomb until he was over the North Channel. Then the salt water went for his sinuses and his respiration breathing was done for.'

And when the bird took over sixteen hours to return from Wexford on a day that was calm and clear and sunny Handme said, 'Harry, I've got the answer now. He's tired of the wee hen! Give him another hen and you'll find he'll be back before he leaves!'

'He wouldn't be interested in another hen,' said Harry.

'He wouldn't what?' said Handme, baring his teeth. 'Pigeons are no different to the rest of us!'

'For your information,' said Harry, remembering a quotation from the *Post,* ' "Pigeons tend to be monogamous." '

'Is that what Father Mendel says?'

'It is,' said Harry wearily.

'You may be sure! That's what's wrong with us in this country – bloody-well priest-ridden! And, if you ask me, he should know nothing about all that. So take my advice, Harry, and get him another mate.'

'It's in him,' said Harry, not answering the tailor. 'It's deep down in him. All I need is time. Because it's deep down in him.'

The Fusilier was of the opinion that the bird was physically perfect but that some delicate imbalance in its psyche caused it to have momentary blackouts when it was on the wing. All birds, he explained to Judith, depended for their direction on the action of the earth's magnetic grid on the membrane of the mind. It had to do with electricity and electrodes, he said. And when Harry's cock was flying it suffered from 'mental blackouts, like blown fuses', so that it had to fly blind for periods until the psyche righted itself. Something similar happened to men suffering from shell shock, he believed.

With great peals of laughter Judith relayed this information to Harry at lunch one Sunday. Ever since his mother had become invalided he had taken his Sunday meals with her.

'Rubbish!' he said, his tears dropping into the rhubarb pie.

'It sounded great to me,' she said.

'All lies,' he grunted.

'Well, can you explain how your birds know how to make their way home over hundreds of miles?'

'Course I can,' he said. 'It's based on science.'

'Science?'

'Every bird has a microscopic eye,' he said patiently. 'What's the first thing he does when he is liberated? He gets away up into the sky and looks about him. With his two eyes – the kind you and me have – he gets his bearings. But with his microscopic eye – it's buried inside his skull – he sort of takes a photograph of the whole country, like a bloody big map in his head. He knows then exactly where he is and plots his course according.'

'Not a doubt in the world?'

'As simple as if he were running on railway lines.'

'Lucky bird,' said Judith. 'Lucky, lucky bird.'

For a second he wondered at the tone of her voice. But almost at once she was laughing again and telling him that she had had a letter from Billy in Canada. He had married, got himself a good job, and wanted her to join him.

'With the microscopic eye,' said Harry, 'it's as simple as running on railway lines.'

The All-Ireland Open Championship was held on Saturday,

August 5th. All birds had to be at the liberating station, Mizen Head, County Cork, by nine o'clock the night before. They would be released the following morning at ten, weather conditions being clement and propitious, as the *Post* put it.

Major O'Donnell volunteered to take all the Mullaghduff entrants in his beach wagon to Mizen Head on Friday. There were seven local competitors: Joe McSorley's checkered hen; the Major's two yearlings; Patsy Boyle's old grey hen, her daughter, and her granddaughter; and Harry's cock. The Major sent word to Harry that he would call for the cock after lunch.

That morning Harry was a mass of nerves. He spilled a bucket of maize on the floor of the loft and when he was down on his hands and knees, gathering it up, he cracked his head on the handle of the door. The birds sensed his anxiety and flew recklessly from side to side, cooing, colliding, squabbling, injuring themselves. All except the blue-grey cock. He stood quietly beneath the trap, now on one foot, now on the other, blinking his eyes, waiting.

Judith came panting up the stairs. 'Harry! Harry, where are you?'

'Up here! In the loft!'

She climbed the remaining stairs. 'The Major's below,' she gasped, 'looking for the basket.'

'He's what? Sure, it's not lunchtime yet!'

'It's almost two o'clock,' she said. 'Come on. Here's the basket. Where's the bird?'

'The bird's not ready. I haven't ringed him yet and he's not washed, and he has to –'

'Give me,' she said, plucking the rubber band from his hand. 'This is him, isn't it?'

'That's – Easy! Easy! Handle him gently!'

She picked up the pigeon, turned him over on his back, and slipped the ring over his left foot.

37

'Now, give him to me,' said Harry. 'I still have to wash him down.'

'You haven't time,' she said briskly. 'The Major won't wait. Where's the red hen?'

Harry pointed to a nest with a wire-mesh door.

Judith opened the door and put the cock in with the hen. She closed the door again.

The cock spread his wings and arched his neck.

'That's enough,' said Harry. 'Take him out.'

'Leave them!' she said with quiet authority, as if the loft was hers and not his.

The other birds settled on their perches and went suddenly still.

The hen got to her feet. The cock began beating the mesh with his wings.

'Quick!' Harry snapped. 'Before it's too late!'

'Leave them,' she said softly, staring at them.

'For God's sake, woman, if you let him go on he won't come back. He won't race!'

'Leave them,' she said again, in a whisper.

'You'll ruin everything! You don't understand –'

'Leave them!'

The hen squatted on the floor. The cock found his balance.

For a second there was no sound. Then suddenly, violently, Harry pushed her aside. 'By God, I won't!' he shouted. He flung open the door and grabbed the cock. The whole loft went mad again.

'You don't understand, woman,' he said, thrusting the bird into the basket and talking rapidly to atone for his violence. 'If you let him go on he would never come back. For God's sake, that's the meaning of the widowhood system – to get him to come back. You don't understand these things. They're natural – natural and scientific. Look, he's bustin' to get back to her already! That's what it means, the widowhood system, d'you see?'

'It's a queer system,' she said in a dreamy way, still staring into the cage.

'Look at him! Searching for her! Sure, it's the most natural thing in the world. Just because he can't get her. But if you were to leave them together for a week, by God, he wouldn't fly the length of himself to join her! Funny, isn't it?'

'The Major's waiting,' she said, turning away from the red hen and going to the top of the stairs.

He lifted the basket and followed her.

The Major took the bird, put it into the back of his beach wagon, and drove off. Harry and she stood together at the edge of the pavement and watched the car disappear round the corner.

'How d'you think it'll do?' he said at last.

She lifted her smooth, round face and looked up at him. 'He's bound to come back to her, isn't he?' she asked.

'He'll come back, all right. But it's the time he does it in that matters to me.'

'But he'll always come back, looking for her?'

'Naturally!'

'Searching for her?'

'Provided you don't let them mate first – like you were just going to do,' he said, laughing.

'I hope you're right, Harry,' she said, her hazel eyes looking at something beyond his face.

He sensed her abstraction, a solemnity in her stillness. 'Come on inside,' he said uneasily, because Judith was strange to him when she was not laughing. 'I want you to put a patch on my head.'

Together they went into the shop.

The following morning was blue and fragile but by afternoon the sky became overcast and a drizzle of rain glazed the streets and rooftops. Even if the bird were to do the two-hundred-and-eighty-one miles from Mizen Head in eight hours Harry calculated – and to beat McSorley's hen it would have to do at least that – it would not arrive back in Mullaghduff until six that evening. But every quarter-of-an-hour after he had made his lunch he found himself running from the shop to the loft and back again to the shop. Eventually he closed the shop altogether and joined Handme and the Fusilier in the loft.

He would have been wiser to stay in the shop because their calm – worse, their assumption that the cock would never make its way back in such weather – unnerved him altogether.

'Ah, well,' sighed Handme, 'it's a lesson to us all. If he had been a hen now . . .'

'There's no comparison,' said the Fusilier. 'Like greyhounds and whippets.'

'The wind and the rain might do their damnedest on him,' Handme went on, 'but he would make it back to the nest, come hell or high water. Nature is a wonderful invention.'

'But he's a cock,' said the Fusilier.

'A strong cock, not a bad cock at all, but still a cock,' said Handme. The details of the bird's possible loss interested him. 'Would he even have made the length of Limerick?' he asked the Fusilier.

'At the very outside,' said the Fusilier.

'If the north-Cork hawks didn't get him first.'

'Bad brutes, them.'

'They've been known to attack children – even north-Cork children.'

'Or maybe he broke his neck on the telegraph wires.'

'All the same the spirit would have been game enough.'

'He had spirit; I'll say that for him.'

'And staying power.'

'But a cock,' said the Fusilier.

'A good cock, but still a cock.'

'Give me the natural system every time.'

'That's what's wrong with the widowhood system,' said Handme. 'It's just not natural.'

Harry watched the rain blacken the trunks of the pine trees. 'It's in him,' he muttered. 'It's deep down in him.'

'What's that, Harry?' asked the Fusilier.

Harry turned round. 'Go in next door,' he said, 'and tell Judith to make us a pot of tea. We have a couple of hours to wait yet.'

'And get us some refreshments when you're out!' Handme called after the Fusilier.

'The All-Ireland Open must be a wonderful sight,' Handme went on. 'To see five or six thousand birds being liberated at the one time.' He licked his lips and bared his teeth until the gums showed. 'Man, it's something I dream about. A lovely summer morning, and ten thousand fluttering angels rising up to heaven and painting the celestial sky with white and grey and –'

'D'you know what I dream about?' snapped Harry. 'That some day you'll pay me the seven months' rent you owe me!'

Handme lowered his head and Harry went back to the traps and stared out at the rain. Even the birds went silent, squatting motionless on the perches, watching.

The Fusilier came back with two dozen stout and the news that Judith was not at home.

'Of course she's in. She's always in on a Saturday afternoon,' said Harry.

'I'm telling you she's not,' said the Fusilier. 'Go and see for yourself. Anyhow, the gas man's down there, looking to read your meter.'

Harry saw to the gas man and then went into Judith's house. It was empty. He went through the narrow hall, into the kitchen, and out to the back garden, calling, 'Judith! Are you home, Judith?' He stood at the bottom of the stairs and called up, 'Judith! Judith?' There was no reply.

Then, for no reason at all except that the race had upset him, the thought suddenly struck him that maybe she was lying dying across the bed. He tore up the stairs and flung open the bedroom door. The room was empty. Only her pink nightdress lay across the bottom of the bed. His calm returned. He came downstairs again, pulled the front door after him, and went back to his own house. Before he went up to the loft he took a handkerchief from the row that was drying in front of the range in the kitchen because his eyes were giving him hell.

By the time the bottles were finished Handme and the Fusilier had discussed politics, the Church, and the decline in public morals. Harry heard them but did not listen. He was battling north with his bird, fighting wind and rain and telegraph poles and hawks. His microscopic eye was not functioning and he was flying by instinct, doggedly, over wet black bogs and dirty lakes and sodden fields, uncertain if he was going in the right direction but determined to carry on. The terrible effort anaesthetized him; his mind was numb. The labour of keeping his cock aloft and flying and of magnetizing it to himself exhausted him.

'She might,' he heard the Fusilier saying.

'It would be the sensible thing to do,' said Handme.

Dusk was falling. The birds were making their settling-in night noises.

'She's still a strong young woman,' said Handme.

'And they say Canada's a fine country,' said the Fusilier.

'She'll go, all right,' said Handme.

Harry dried his eyes. 'Go where?' he asked. 'Who?'

'I'm just telling the Fusilier here that Judith's thinking of joining the brother in Canada.'

'How do you know that?' said Harry. His mind was stirring again. The exhaustion was melting from his body.

'She was telling me herself.'

'What about a drink, boys?' the Fusilier broke in. 'Do you feel like going out for some, Harry?'

'Yes,' said Harry. 'Yes – Yes, I'll go and get some.'

As he was leaving the loft Handme was saying, 'With all this automation and stuff what in God's name will men do with their leisure time? That's what worries me.'

The smirking dummies in Handme's living room leered at Harry as he passed them, and whispered, 'Canada! Canada! Canada!' Their soft, insinuating voices followed him down to the ground floor.

'Like hell!' he said aloud to himself. 'Like bloody hell!' But the sound of his own voice, unechoed, unanswered, only aggravated the fear that was growing in him.

Slowly, controlling his steps, refusing to be panicked, he walked into the house next door.

'Judith!' he called sternly. Then again, 'Judith!'

When no reply came his fears babbled to him excitedly. 'She's gone to Billy in Canada!' He saw her again as she stood in the loft watching the cock and the hen. He heard her ask, 'He'll always come back, looking for her?'

He came out into the street and stood in the rain, and again tried to will his frightened mind into silence. But it would not be still. It drove him into motion, moving his legs, slowly at first, then urging him forward more and more quickly, until he was trotting along Distillery Lane and out the Dublin road towards the glove factory. Of course she was not there. It was the half day; the big iron gates were locked. Nor was she in the church. Nor was she anywhere about the three streets that met in the square. And by now his brain had ceased functioning again, although his body was still fresh – even vigorous. If the mind had been capable of throwing up any suggestion, however absurd – she had gone to visit cousins in Letterkenny; she had gone shopping to Coleraine – he would have gone there at once. But his mind was comatose and only his stupid body kept going, eagerly, pointlessly. Three times he tried the church; three times he went round the square. And then, exhausted, he came back to her house again.

The door was open. The smell of frying met him in the hall. 'Judith? Judy?'

'Harry?' Her untroubled voice answered from the kitchen.

He closed the door behind him and groped his way through the hall. His tears were blinding him.

From then on he never knew exactly what happened. Afterwards he had a vague memory of catching her plump hands in his and kissing them roughly, of her asking him over and over again, 'Are you sober, Harry? Are you sober?' and of her laughter bubbling, swelling, rising to an unnatural pitch, and then stopping altogether. He just closed his eyes and held her while she poured out a flow of gibberish about how that afternoon his talk of the widowhood system had given her the idea of going away, going anywhere, with the certainty at first that he would come searching for her. And then, when she was wandering along the Strabane road, how that certainty abandoned her, and how she had had to come back. He knew that he had tried to answer her but he could only repeat that he had been running in search of her 'like a bloody pigeon'. He kept saying with incredulity, 'Like a bloody stupid pigeon!'

The only memory of their reunion that would always remain sharp and clear to him was of her whispering to him, at some stage, 'Will you marry me, Harry?' and of himself kissing her on the mouth in love and gratitude, because somehow, at that moment, the question seemed apt. More than apt – inspired.

It was no time to talk of the race, he was aware of that, but that was what he talked of for the next half hour – of the bird's strength and courage and determination; of his confidence that it would make Mullaghduff, maybe not in winning time, but at least completing the course. (And he was right about that, at least; the cock turned up at the loft just after noon the next day.) Talk of the cock led him to Handme and the Fusilier – the big long string and the wee tight keg – sitting in the dusk of the loft, discussing automation, their feet ringed with empty bottles, waiting for replenishments. The more he talked of them the funnier they seemed to be. Never before had they seemed funny. After all they were his friends, his best friends. But now, for the first time, he saw them in another way and they were ludicrous — two middle-aged men wasting their lives waiting for a pigeon to come home! He began to chuckle. The chuckle grew into a laugh. In the end he was laughing so that his sides hurt and his eyes were streaming with water. And in the crook of his arm Judith was laughing, too, and crying, too. And for that half hour, for all the crying, they were the happiest couple in the whole of Mullaghduff.

The Potato Gatherers

November frost had starched the flat countryside into silent rigidity. The 'rat-tat-tat' of the tractor's exhaust drilled into the clean, hard air but did not penetrate it; each staccato sound broke off as if it had been nipped. Hunched over the driver's wheel sat Kelly, the owner, a rock of a man with a huge head and broken fingernails, and in the trailer behind were his four potato gatherers – two young men, permanent farmhands, and the two boys he had hired for the day. At six o'clock in the morning they were the only living things in that part of County Tyrone.

The boys chatted incessantly. They stood at the front of the trailer, legs apart, hands in their pockets, their faces pressed forward into the icy rush of air, their senses edged for perception. Joe, the elder of the two – he was thirteen and had worked for Kelly on two previous occasions – might have been quieter, but his brother's excitement was infectious. For this was Philly's first job, his first time to take a day off from school to earn money, his first opportunity to prove that he was a man at twelve years of age. His energy was a burden to him. Behind them, on the floor of the trailer, the two farmhands lay sprawled in half sleep.

Twice the boys had to cheer. The first time was when they were passing Dicey O'Donnell's house and Philly, who was in the same class as Dicey, called across to the thatched, smokeless building, 'Remember me to all the boys, Dicey!' The second time was when they came to the school itself. It was then that Kelly turned to them and growled to them to shut up.

'Do you want the whole county to know you're taking the day off?' he said. 'Save your breath for your work.'

When Kelly faced back to the road ahead Philly stuck his thumbs in his ears, put out his tongue, and wriggled his fingers at the back of Kelly's head. Then, suddenly forgetting him, he said, 'Tell me, Joe, what are you going to buy?'

'Buy?'

'With the money we get today. I know what I'm getting – a shotgun. Bang! Bang! Bang! Right there, mistah. Jist you put yer two hands up above yer head and I reckon you'll live a little longer.' He menaced Kelly's neck.

'Agh!' said Joe derisively.

'True as God, Joe. I can get it for seven shillings – an old one that's lying in Tom Tracey's father's barn. Tom told me he would sell it for seven shillings.'

'Who would sell it?'

'Tom.'

'Steal it, you mean. From his old fella.'

'His old fella has a new one. This one's not wanted.' He sighted along an imaginary barrel and picked out an unsuspecting sparrow in the hedge. 'Bang! Never knew what hit you, did you? What are you going to buy, Joe?'

'I don't know. There won't be much to buy with. Maybe – naw, I don't know. Depends on what Ma gives us back.'

'A bicycle, Joe. What about a bike? Quinn would give his away for a packet of cigarettes. You up on the saddle, Joe, and me on the crossbar. Out to the millrace every evening. Me shooting all the rabbits along the way. Bang! Bang! Bang! What about a bike, Joe?'

'I don't know. I don't know.'

'What did she give you back the last time?'

'I can't remember.'

'Ten shillings? More? What did you buy then? A leather belt? A set of rabbit snares?'

'I don't think I got anything back. Maybe a shilling. I don't remember.'

'A shilling! One lousy shilling out of fourteen! Do you know what I'm going to buy?' He hunched his shoulders and lowered his head between them, one eye closed in a huge wink. 'Tell no one? Promise?'

'What?'

'A gaff. See?'

'What about the gun?'

'It can wait until next year. But a gaff, Joe. See? Old Philly down there beside the Black Pool. A big salmon. A beaut. Flat on my belly, and – *phwist!* – there he is on the bank, the gaff stuck in his guts.' He clasped his middle and writhed in agony, imitating the fish. Then his act switched suddenly back to cowboys and he drew from both holsters at a cat sneaking home along the hedge. 'Bang! Bang! That sure settled you, boy. Where *is* this potato territory, mistah? Ah want to show you hombres what work is. What's a-keeping this old tractor-buggy?'

'We're jist about there, Mistah Philly, sir,' said Joe. 'Ah reckon you'll show us, OK. You'll show us.'

The field was a two-acre rectangle bordered by a low hedge. The ridges of potatoes stretched lengthwise in straight, black lines. Kelly unfastened the trailer and hooked up the mechanical digger. The two labourers stood with their hands in their pockets and scowled around them, cigarettes hanging from their lips.

'You two take the far side,' Kelly told them. 'And Joe, you and –' He could not remember the name. 'You and the lad there, you two take this side. You show him what to do, Joe.' He climbed up on the tractor seat. 'And remember,' he called over his shoulder, 'if the school attendance officer appears it's up to you to run. I never seen you. I never heard of you.'

The tractor moved forward into the first ridges, throwing up a spray of brown earth behind it as it went.

'Right,' said Joe. 'What we do is this, Philly. When the digger passes we gather the spuds into these buckets and then carry the buckets to the sacks and fill them. Then back again to fill the buckets. And back to the sacks. OK, mistah?'

'OK, mistah. Child's play. What does he want four of us for? I could do the whole field myself – one hand tied behind my back.'

Joe smiled at him. 'Come on, then. Let's see you.'

'Just you watch,' said Philly. He grabbed a bucket and ran stumbling across the broken ground. His small frame bent over the clay and his thin arms worked madly. Before Joe had begun gathering Philly's voice called to him. 'Joe! Look! Full already! Not bad, eh?'

'Take your time,' Joe called back.

'And look, Joe! Look!' Philly held his hands out for his brother's inspection. They were coated with earth. 'How's that, Joe? They'll soon be as hard as Kelly's!'

Joe laughed. 'Take it easy, Philly. No rush.'

But Philly was already stooped again over his work and when Joe was emptying his first bucket into the sack Philly was emptying his third. He gave Joe the huge wink again and raced off.

Kelly turned at the bottom of the field and came back up. Philly was standing waiting for him.

'What you need is a double digger, Mr Kelly!' he called as the tractor passed. But Kelly's eyes never left the ridges in front of him. A flock of seagulls swooped and dipped behind the tractor, fluttering down to catch worms in the newly turned earth. The boy raced off with his bucket.

'How's it going?' shouted Joe after another twenty minutes. Philly was too busy to answer.

A pale sun appeared about 8.30. It was not strong enough to soften the earth but it loosened sounds – cars along the road, birds in the naked trees, cattle let out for the day. The clay became damp under it but did not thaw. The tractor exulted in its new freedom and its splutterings filled the countryside.

'I've been thinking,' said Philly when he met Joe at a sack. 'Do you know what I'm going to get, Joe? A scout knife with one of those leather scabbards. Four shillings in Byrne's shop. Great for skinning a rabbit.' He held his hands out from his sides now because they were raw in places. 'Yeah. A scout knife with a leather scabbard.'

'A scout knife,' Joe repeated.

'You always have to carry a scout knife in case your gun won't fire or your powder gets wet. And when you're swimming underwater you can always carry a knife between your teeth.'

'We'll have near twenty ridges done before noon,' said Joe.

'He should have a double digger. I told him that. Too slow, mistah. Too doggone slow. Tell me, Joe, have you made up your mind yet?'

'What about?'

'What you're going to buy, stupid.'

'Aw, naw. Naw – I don't know yet.'

Philly turned to his work again and was about to begin when the school bell rang. He dropped his bucket and danced back to his brother. 'Listen! Joe! Listen!' He caught fistfuls of his hair and tugged his head from side to side. 'Listen! Listen! Ha, ha, ha! Ho, ho, ho! Come on, you fat, silly, silly scholars and get to your lessons! Come on, come on, come on, come on! No dallying! Speed it up! Get a move on! Hurry! Hurry! Hurry! "And where are the O'Boyle brothers today? Eh? Where are they? Gathering potatoes? What's that I hear? What? What?"'

'Look out, lad!' roared Kelly.

The tractor passed within inches of Philly's legs. He jumped out of its way in time but a fountain of clay fell on his head and shoulders. Joe ran to his side.

'Are you all right, Philly? Are you OK?'

'Tried to get me, that's what he did, the dirty cattle thief. Tried to get me.'

'You OK, mistah? Reckon you'll live?'

'Sure, mistah. Take more 'n that ole coyote to scare me. Come on, mistah. We'll show him what men we really are.' He shook his jacket and hair and hitched up his trousers. 'Would you swap now, Joe?'

'Swap what?'

'Swap places with those poor eejits back there?' He jerked his thumb in the direction of the school.

'No, sir,' said Joe. 'Not me.'

'Nor me neither, mistah. Meet you in the saloon.' He swaggered off, holding his hands as if they were delicate things, not part of him.

They broke for lunch at noon. By then the sun was high and brave but still of little use. With the engine of the tractor cut off for a brief time there was a self-conscious silence which became relaxed and natural when the sparrows, now audible, began to chirp. The seagulls squabbled over the latest turned earth and a cautious puff of wind stirred the branches of the tall trees. Kelly adjusted the digger while he ate. On the far side of the field the two labourers stretched themselves on sacks and conversed in monosyllables. Joe and Philly sat on upturned buckets. For lunch they each had half a scone of homemade soda bread cut into thick slices and skimmed with butter. They washed it down with mouthfuls of cold tea from a bottle. After they had eaten Joe threw the crusts to the gulls, gathered up the newspapers in which the bread had been wrapped, emptied out the remains of the tea, and put the bottle and the papers into his jacket pocket. Then he stood up and stretched himself.

'My back's getting stiff,' he said.

Philly sat with his elbows on his knees and studied the palms of his hands.

'Sore?' asked Joe.

'What?'

'Your hands. Are they hurting you?'

'They're OK,' said Philly. 'Tough as leather. But the clay's sore. Gets right into every cut and away up your nails.' He held his arms out. 'They're shaking,' he said. 'Look.'

'That's the way they go,' said Joe. 'But they'll – Listen! Do you hear?'

'Hear what?'

'Lunchtime at school. They must be playing football in the playground.'

The sounds of high, delighted squealing came intermittently when the wind sighed. They listened to it with their heads uplifted, their faces broadening with memory.

'We'll get a hammering tomorrow,' said Joe. 'Six on each hand.'

'It's going to be a scout knife,' Philly said. 'I've decided on that.'

'She mightn't give us anything back. Depends on how much she needs herself.'

'She said she would. She promised. Have you decided yet?'

'I'm still thinking,' said Joe.

The tractor roared suddenly, scattering every other sound.

'Come on, mistah,' said the older one. 'Four more hours to go. Saddle up your horse.'

'Coming. Coming,' Philly replied. His voice was sharp with irritation.

The sun was a failure. It held its position in the sky and flooded the countryside with light but could not warm it. Even before it had begun to slip to the west the damp ground had become glossy again, and before the afternoon was spent patches of white frost were appearing on higher ground. Now the boys were working automatically, their minds acquiescing in what their bodies did. They no longer straightened up; the world was their feet and the hard clay and the potatoes and their hands and the buckets and the sacks. Their ears told them where the tractor was, at the bottom of the field, turning, approaching.

Their muscles had become adjusted to their stooped position and, as long as the boys kept within the established pattern of movement, their arms and hands and legs and shoulders seemed to float as if they were free of gravity. But if something new was expected from the limbs – a piece of glass to be thrown into the hedge, a quick stepping back to avoid the digger – then their bodies shuddered with pain and the tall trees reeled and the hedges rose to the sky.

Dicey O'Donnell gave them a shout from the road on his way home from school. 'Hi! Joe! Philly!'

They did not hear him. He waited until the tractor turned. 'Hi! Hi! Philly! Philly! Joe!'

'Youse are for it the morrow. I'm telling youse. He knows where youse are. He says he's going to beat the scruff out of youse the morrow. Youse are in for it, all right. Blue murder! Bloody hell! True as God!'

'Get lost!' Joe called back.

'Aye, and he's going to report youse to the attendance officer, and your old fella'll be fined. Youse are ruined! Destroyed! Blue murder!'

'Will I put a bullet in him, mistah?' said Joe to Philly.

Philly did not answer. He thought he was going to fall and his greatest fear was that he might fall in front of the tractor, because now the tractor's exhaust had only one sound, fixed forever in his head, and unless he saw the machine he could not tell whether it was near him or far away. The 'rat-tat-tat' was a finger tapping in his head, drumming at the back of his eyes.

'Vamoose, O'Donnell!' called Joe. 'You annoy us. Vamoose.'

O'Donnell said something more about the reception they could expect the next day, but he got tired of calling to two stooped backs and he went off home.

The last pair of ridges was turned when the sky had veiled itself for dusk. The two brothers and the two labourers worked on until they met in the middle. Now the field was all brown, all flat, except for the filled sacks that patterned it. Kelly was satisfied; his lips formed an *O* and he blew through them as if he were trying to whistle. He detached the digger and hooked up the trailer. 'All aboard!' he shouted, in an effort at levity.

On the way home the labourers seemed to be fully awake for the first time since morning. They stood in the trailer where the boys had stood at dawn, behind Kelly's head and facing the road before them. They chatted and guffawed and made plans for a dance that night. When they met people they knew along the way they saluted extravagantly. At the crossroads they began to wrestle and Kelly had to tell them to watch out or they would fall over the side. But he did not sound angry.

Joe sat on the floor, his legs straight out before him, his back resting against the side of the trailer. Philly lay flat out, his head cushioned on his brother's lap. Above him the sky spread out, grey, motionless, enigmatic. The warmth from Joe's body made him drowsy. He wished the journey home to go on forever, the sound of the tractor engine to anaesthetize his mind forever. He knew that if the movement and the sound were to cease the pain of his body would be unbearable.

'We're nearly there,' said Joe quietly. 'Are you asleep?' Philly did not answer. 'Mistah! Are you asleep, mistah?'

'No.'

Darkness came quickly, and when the last trace of light disappeared the countryside became taut with frost. The head-lamps of the tractor glowed yellow in the cold air.

'Philly? Are you awake, mistah?'

'What?'

'I've been thinking,' said Joe slowly. 'And do you know what I think? I think I've made up my mind now.'

One of the labourers burst into song.

' "If I were a blackbird I'd whistle and sing, and I'd follow the ship that my true love sails in." '

His mate joined him at the second line and their voices exploded in the stiff night.

'Do you know what I'm going to buy?' Joe said, speaking more loudly. 'If she gives us something back, that is. Mistah! Mistah Philly! Are you listening? I'm going to buy a pair of red silk socks.'

He waited for approval from Philly. When none came he reshook his brother's head. 'Do you hear, mistah? Red silk socks – the kind Jojo Teague wears. What about that, eh? What do you think?'

Philly stirred and half raised his head from his brother's lap. 'I think you're daft,' he said in an exhausted, sullen voice. 'Ma won't give us back enough to buy anything much. No more than a shilling. You knew it all the time.' He lay down again and in a moment he was fast asleep.

Joe held his brother's head against the motion of the trailer and repeated the words 'red silk socks' to himself again and again, nodding each time at the wisdom of his decision.

Mr Sing My Heart's Delight

On the first day of every new year I made the forty-five-mile journey by train, mail car, and foot across County Donegal to my granny's house which sat at the top of a cliff above the raging Atlantic at the very end of the parish of Mullaghduff. This annual visit, lasting from January until the nights began to shorten some time in March, was made primarily for Granny's benefit: during those months Grandfather went across to Scotland to earn enough money to tide them over the rest of the year. But it suited me admirably too: I missed school for three months, I got away from strict parents and bothersome brothers and sisters, all younger than I, and in Granny's house I was cock-of-the-walk and everything I did was right.

The house consisted of one room in which Granny and Grandfather lived and slept. It was a large room lit by a small window and a door which could be left open for the greater part of the day because it faced east and the winds usually blew from the west. There were three chairs, a table, a bed in the corner, a dresser, and an open hearth fire over which stretched the mantelpiece, the focal point of the room. In such bare surroundings that mantelpiece held a rich array. A china dog stood guard at each end and between them there was a shining silver alarm clock, two vases, a brass elf holding a cracked thermometer whose mercury had long since been spilled, a golden picture frame enclosing a coloured photograph of a race horse, and the shells of three sea urchins sitting on three matchboxes covered with red crêpe paper. Every year I went there I had to have each of those pieces handed down to me for examination and appraisal and my pleasure in them made them even more precious to Granny.

She herself was a small, plump woman who must have been petite and very pretty. She always dressed in black – boots, woollen stockings, overall – a dark, inelegant black, turning grey with too much washing and too much exposure to the weather. But above the neck she was a surprise of strong colour: white hair, sea-blue eyes, and a quick, fresh face, tanned deep with sun. When something delighted her she had a habit of wagging her head rapidly from side to side like a precocious child with ringlets and although she was over sixty then she behaved like a woman half that age. Indeed, when I felt tired or lazy and she would challenge me to race her to the byre or dare me to go beyond her along the rocks at low water, I used to tell her that she was 'nothing but a giddy, feather-headed old woman', repeating what I had heard my mother say of her so often.

Even on the best day in summer Mullaghduff is a desolate place. The land is rocky, barren, uneven, covered by a brown heather that never blooms, and hacked into a crazy jigsaw by hundreds of tiny rivulets no more than a foot wide which seem to flow in as many different directions and yet cunningly avoid crossing one another. Granny's house lay at the most inaccessible end of this vast waste, three miles from the nearest road. It was a strange place to make a home but Grandfather was a dour, silent man and he probably felt that, by marrying the girl of seventeen who had an infant daughter but no father to claim it, he had shown sufficient charity: the least she could do was accept the terms of his proposal. Or perhaps he was jealous of her vivacity and attractiveness and thought that the wide Atlantic behind her and a three-mile stretch of moor before her would be good deterrents to a roaming spirit. Whatever his motives, he succeeded in cutting her off so completely from the world that at the time of her death, shortly after my thirteenth birthday, the longest journey she had ever made was to the town of Strabane, fifty-two miles away, and that journey she had made the month before her marriage to fix up legal documents in connection with her baby, my mother.

She and I had riotous times together. We laughed with one another and at one another. (A constant source of fun was Granny's English. Irish was her first tongue and she never felt at ease in English which she shouted and spat out as if it were getting in her way.) We used to sit up until near midnight, chatting and gossiping and then, instead of going to bed, perhaps decide suddenly to feast ourselves on herring fried in butter or on sand eels roasted on the red coals or on a wild duck that was for the next day's dinner. Or we would huddle round the fire and I would read to her stories from my school reading book – she could neither read nor write. She would listen avidly to these, her face keen with interest, not missing a word, making me go back over a paragraph which she did not fully understand or halting me with a question about some detail in the story.

'Were you in a bus ever? A real bus – for people?'

'Once.'

'What was it like, what? Was it bad on the stomach, was it?'

Or, after reading, she herself would retell the story to me ('Just to see did I understand it right') especially if it was a tale about the daring of the lighthouse-keeper's daughter or a cameo biography of someone like Madame Curie or Florence Nightingale. And then the greed for knowledge about the outside world would fall away as quickly from her and she would jump to her feet and say, 'Christ, son, we near forgot!' She used this swear word without any suggestion of profanity and because, I believe now, she rarely heard the conversation of women of her own time. 'If we run to the lower rocks we'll see the Norwegian fishing boats going round the point. Hurry, son, hurry! They're a sight on a good night. Hurry!'

Out there on the rump of Mullaghduff she had no ready-made entertainments to amuse me but she thought nothing of her own discomfort to make my stay with her more interesting. We often rose before dawn to see wild geese spearing through the icy air high above the ocean. Or we sat for hours at a stretch on the flat rocks below her house to get a glimpse of sharks encircling an oily patch that betrayed a shoal of mackerel and then attacking it. Or we waded knee-deep in water at the shallow strand and felt the terrible thrill of fluke wriggling beneath our bare feet, closed our eyes and plunged our hands down to lift them out. I know now that all these little expeditions were thought up to amuse me but I am also certain that, once we had embarked on them, Granny enjoyed them every bit as much as I did.

'Christ, it's a calf I have under my foot and not a fluke at all!' she would squeal with nervous delight, her blue eyes radiant with joy. 'Come here, son! Come here and steady the arm of me!'

Or if we were standing on top of the hump of ground behind her house to get a good view of a passing transatlantic liner, all sequins of lights, she would fill it for me with a passenger list of gay, carefree people: 'Lords and ladies,' she would say. 'The men of them handsome and straight as heroes and the women of them in bright silks down to their toes and all of them laughing and dancing and drinking wine and singing. Christ, son, but they're a happy old cargo!'

There was a February gale blowing in from the sea the evening the packman battled his way up to us. I watched him through the kitchen window, a shrub in the middle of the bog, only it was bending against the wind. Then it grew to a man and then a man with a cardboard case half as big as himself. When he was a stone's throw from the door I saw that he was coloured. In those days packmen were fairly common in remote areas. They went from house to house with their packs or cases of clothes and socks and bed linens and tablecloths and gaudy knick-knacks and if a customer had no money for the goods chosen the packmen were usually willing to settle for the value in poultry or fish. They had the name of being sharp dealers, dishonest even.

The sight of this packman put the fear of God in me because Mother had taught us to be wary of all packmen and I had never seen a coloured man before in my life. I led Granny to the window and peeped out from behind her.

'Will he attack us?' I whimpered.

'Christ, and if he does he'll meet his match in this house!' she said bravely and threw open the door. 'Come in, lad,' she roared into the storm. 'Come in and rest yourself for no goat could have made the climb up here today but a fool like yourself.'

He backed into the kitchen, dragging his huge case after him. He dropped into a chair at the door and his head fell back to a resting position against the wall. His breath came in quick, short gasps and he made no effort to speak he was so exhausted.

I took a step closer to him to examine him. He was a young man, no more than twenty, with a smooth, hazel skin that was a tight fit for his face. The crown of his head was swathed in a snow-white turban, wound round like a bandage. His shoulders were narrow, his body puny, his trousers frayed and wet from the long grass, and his feet as small as my younger sister's. Then I saw his hands. They were fine and delicate and the fingers tipped with pink nails as polished as fresh seaweed. On the third finger of his left hand was a ring. It was a gold ring, wrought in imitation of a snake which held between its mouth and tail a damson-coloured stone. As I watched it the colour became vaporous, like smoke in a bottle, and seemed to writhe languidly in a coiling movement. Now it was purple, now rose, now black, now blood red, now blue, now the colour of sloes in the August sun. I was still gazing at its miracles when the packman slid to his knees on the ground and began reciting in a low, droning voice, 'I sell beau-ti-ful things, good lady; everything to adorn your beau-ti-ful home. What is it you buy? Leenens, silks, sheets, beau-ti-ful pictures for your walls, beau-ti-ful cardigans for the lady. What is it you buy?'

As he spoke he opened his case and removed all its contents, painting the floor with yellows and greens and whites and blues. He did not offer any one item but displayed everything as if for his own gratification – and no wonder, for he owned all the riches of the earth.

'You buy, good lady? What is it you buy?' he intoned without interest, without enthusiasm, but by rote, because he was tired beyond caring. His eyes never left the ground and his hands spread the splashes of colour out and around him until he was an island in a lake of brightness.

For a moment Granny said nothing. She was dazzled by the packman's wares and at the same time she was trying desperately not to miss whatever it was he was saying and his accent was difficult for her. When at last words came to her they broke from her in a sort of cry.

'Aw, Christ, sweet Christ, look at them! Look at them! Aw, God, what is there like them things!' Then rapidly to me, 'What is he saying, son, what? Tell me what it is he's saying.' Then to the packman, 'Mister, I don't speak English too good, mister. Aw, Christ, mister, but they're grand treasures, mister, grand.'

She dropped to the floor beside him and stretched her hands out as if in benediction over the goods. Then her arms went gently down and the tips of her fingers brushed over the surfaces of the garments. She went silent with awe and her mouth opened. Only her eyes were quick with ecstasy.

'Try them on, good lady. Sample what I have to sell.'

She turned to me to confirm that she had heard correctly.

'Put on the things you like,' I said. 'Go ahead.'

She looked at the packman, searching his face to see was he in earnest, fearful in case he was not.

'I have no money, Mister Packman. No money.'

As if she had not spoken the packman went on rearranging his colours and did not look up. Only routine was carrying him through.

'Try them on. They are beau-ti-ful. All.'

She hesitated momentarily, poised over the limitless choice.

'Go on,' I said impatiently. 'Hurry up.'

'Everything for the good lady and for her home,' mumbled the packman to the ground. 'Sample what I have to sell.'

She swooped on them as if she were going to devour them. Her fingers found a scarlet blouse which she snatched up and held against her chest. She looked down at it, looked to us for approbation, held it under her chin and smoothed it out against her while her other hand went instinctively to her hair which she gathered back from her face. Then she was absolutely still, waiting for our verdict.

'Beau-ti-ful,' mumbled the packman automatically.

'Beautiful,' I said, anxious to have everything sampled and done with.

'Beautiful,' echoed Granny, softly, slowly, as if she were using the word for the first time.

Then suddenly she was on her feet, towering above us and leaping around the kitchen floor in a wild, mocking dance. 'Christ!' she squealed, 'youse would have me as silly in the head as the two of youse are. Look at me! Look at me! Fit for a palace I am in all my grandeur!'

Then she cut loose altogether. She flung the blouse to the floor and seized a yellow mohair stole which she draped around her shoulders and paraded up and down the floor in time to her own singing. Then she tried on a green hat and then white gloves and then a blue cardigan and then a multicoloured apron, all the time singing or dancing or waving her arms, all the time shaking her head like mad, delighted, embarrassed, drunk with pleasure, completely carried away.

Before she had gone through half of the garments the years put an end to her antics and she flung herself exhausted on top of the bed and let herself go limp. 'Now, mister, you can take the bloody load away,' she panted, 'for I have no money to buy anything.'

Again the packman did not hear her but shuffled his goods with weary patience and said in his dressy way, 'This you like, good lady.' He touched a pair of brass candlesticks. 'Beau-ti-ful. Very cheap. Very, very cheap.' Granny waved her hands in dismissal.

'No money, mister. No money.'

'Or you like this, good lady, this beau-ti-ful picture of the Holy Divine Redeemer. Also very cheap to you, good lady.'

She closed her eyes and shook her head and waited for her energy to return.

'A lovely thing this, kind lady.' His hand happened on a tiny box covered with imitation leather. Inside lay half a dozen apostle spoons. 'These I sell by large numbers. Everybody loved them. I cannot get them enough,' he said without conviction. 'The box to you, good lady, for half price.'

'Shut up!' she snapped with sudden venom, springing up to a sitting position on the bed and scattering the languor that had emanated from the dealer. 'Shut up, Packman! We are poor people here! We have nothing! Shut up!'

The packman's head sank lower to the ground and he began gathering his goods in to him. It was dark now and he fumbled with the catch on his case.

She regretted her outburst at once because she hopped off the bed and began building up the peat fire. 'You'll eat with us, Packman; there'll be hunger on you. We can offer you –' She paused and swung round to me. 'Christ, son, we'll roast the grouse that was to be Sunday's dinner! That's what we'll do. Grouse and praties and butter and buttermilk and soda farls – a feast, by Christ, a feast!' She turned to the packman. 'Can your stomach hold a feast, Packman?'

'Anything, good lady. Anything.'

'A feast it'll be then,' she pronounced. 'A feast and be damned to Sunday.'

She rolled up her sleeves and began setting the table. The

packman closed his case and went to a corner where he merged with the dark.

'Tell me, Packman,' she called to him from her work, 'what do they call you, what?'

'Singh,' he said.

'What?'

'Singh,' he repeated.

'Man, but that's a strange name. Sing. Sing,' she said, feeling the sound on her tongue. 'I'll tell you what I'll call you, Packman,' she went on, 'I'll call you Mr Sing My Heart's Delight! That's what I'll call you – a good, big mouthful. Mr Sing My Heart's Delight!'

'Yes,' he said submissively.

'Now, Mr Sing My Heart's Delight, let the sleep come over you for an hour and when I give you the call there'll be a feast and a festival before your eyes. Close your eyes and sleep, you poor, battered man, you.'

He closed his eyes obediently and, within five minutes, his head had fallen on his chest.

We ate by the light of an oil lamp, Granny at the bottom of the table, me in the middle, and the packman in the place of honour at the top. It must have been a month since he had a square meal because he bolted his food ravenously and did not lift his eyes until his plate was cleaned. Then he sat back in his seat and smiled at us for the first time. He looked boyish now that he was sated.

'Thank you, good lady,' he said. 'A beau-ti-ful meal.'

'You're welcome,' she said. 'May none of us ever want.' She held the bone of the grouse's leg between her fingers and drew patterns on her plate, her head to one side.

'Where do you come from, Mr Sing My Heart's Delight?' Her tone suggested she was beginning a series of questions.

'The Punjab,' he said.

'And where might that be?'

'India, good lady.'

'India,' she repeated. 'Tell me, is India a hot country, is it?'

'Very warm. Very warm and very poor.'

'Very poor,' she said quietly, adding the detail to the picture she was composing in her mind. 'And the oranges and the bananas grow there on trees and there are all classes of fruit and flowers with all the colours of the rainbow in them?'

'Yes,' he said simply, for he was remembering his own picture. 'It is very beau-ti-ful, good lady. Very beau-ti-ful.'

'And the women,' Granny went on, 'do they wear long silk frocks melting down to the ground? And the men, are the men dressed in claret velvet and black shoes with silver buckles?'

He spread his hands and smiled.

'And the women, strolling about in the sun under the orange trees and the sun taking lights out of their hair and the gallant men raising their feathered hats to them and stepping off the roads to let them pass – in the sun – in the Punjab – in the Garden of Eden –' She was away from us as she spoke, leaving us in the draughty, flagged-floor kitchen, listening to the wind ripping up the ocean below us and trying the weaker parts of the thatched roof. The packman's eyes were closed and his head nodded.

'The Garden of Eden,' said Granny again. 'Where the ground isn't treacherous with bits of streams and the land so rocky that even weeds won't settle in it. And you have God's sun in that Punjab place and there is singing and the playing of musical instruments and the children – aye, the children –' The first drops of a shower came down the chimney and sizzled in the fire.

'Christ!' she said, springing to her feet. 'What class of doddering fools of men am I talking to? Up you get, you clowns you, and let me get at the washing-up.'

The packman woke with a start and made for his case.

'And where are you going?' she shouted to him. 'Christ, man, a badger wouldn't face out on a night like this!'

He stopped in the middle of the floor.

'Well?' she said. 'Don't look at me as if you expected a beating. You'll sleep here tonight. There – across the front of the fire. Like a cat,' she ended off with a shout of laughter.

The packman laughed too.

'Now, Mr Sing My Heart's Delight, get out of my road until me and my wee man here gets cleared up.'

By the time we had the dishes finished and fresh peat spread before the fire for the morning it was bedtime. Granny and I slept together in the bed in the corner, a huge, iron bed whose side was always warm from the hearth. She lay next to the wall and I on the outside. Now we retreated to the shadowy end of the room and undressed. Then, with a skip and a jump, we were in the bed together before the packman had time to be embarrassed.

Granny peeped across me. 'Blow out the lamp, Mr Sing My Heart's Delight, and then place yourself on the floor there. You'll find a mat at the door if you want it.'

'Goodnight, good lady,' he said. 'Very good lady.'

'Goodnight, Mr Sing My Heart's Delight,' she replied.

He got the mat and stretched himself out before the red and white embers. Outside the rain lashed against the roof and inside the three of us were as cosy as pet hens.

It was a fine morning, a fresh, blustering day that kept the clouds moving past and dried the path that led from the house to the main road. The packman was young and bright and his case seemed lighter too because he swung it easily by his side as he stood at the door, nodding his head and smiling happily as Granny directed him towards the parishes where he would have the best chance to sell his wares.

'And now,' she said in conclusion, 'God's speed and may the road rise with you.'

'To pay you I have no money, good lady,' said the packman, 'and my worthless goods I would not offer you because –'

'Off with you, man. Off with you. There'll be rain before dinner-time and you should have eight miles behind you by then.' The packman still hesitated. He kept smiling and bowing and swinging his case as if he were a shy girl.

'Christ, Mr Sing My Heart's Delight, if you don't soon go, it's here you'll be for dinner and you ate it last night!'

The packman put his case on the ground and looked at his left hand. Then, drawing off the ring with those long, delicate fingers of his, he held it forward towards her. 'For you,' he said, in a very formal voice. 'Please accept from me in – in grateful.'

Even as it lay on his hand the stone turned a dozen colours. Granny was embarrassed. It had been so long since she had been offered a present that she did not know how to accept it. She hung her head and muttered churlishly, 'No. No. No,' and backed away from the gift.

'But please, good lady. Please,' the packman insisted. 'From a Punjab gentleman to a Donegal lady. A present. Please.'

When she did not come forward to accept it he moved towards her and caught her hand in his. He chose the third finger of the left hand and slipped the ring on it. 'Thank you, good lady,' he said.

Then he lifted his case, bowed to us again and turned towards the barren waste and the main road. The wind was behind him and carried him quickly away.

Neither of us moved until we had lost him behind the hillock at the bend of the road. I turned to go round to the side of the house: it was time to let the hens out and milk the cow. But Granny did not move. She stood looking towards the road with her arm and hand still held as the packman had left them.

'Come on, Granny,' I said irritably. 'The cow will think we're dead.'

She looked strangely at me and then away from me and across the bogs and the road and up towards the mountains which almost surrounded her.

'Come on, Granny,' I said, tugging at her overall. 'Come on. Come on.'

She allowed me to pull her; and as I led her towards the byre I heard her saying to herself, 'I'm thinking the rain will get him this side of Crolly Bridge and the claret breeches and the buckled shoes will be destroyed on him. Please God it will make a good day of it. Please God it will.'

My Father and the Sergeant

If you turn west outside the town of Drumkill in the County of Tyrone and follow the narrow, rising road to its end five miles away you will find yourself in the townland of Knockenagh where my father taught school for the whole of his restless life and where I was born and reared. It is a shelf of arable land buttressing the face of the grey-black mountains that keep County Tyrone and County Donegal apart from one another. From the door of our house or, better still, from the door of the schoolhouse fifty yards further up the mountain we could see right across the patchwork of meticulous fields to the town itself which was always lazy in sunlight. We called it 'sunny Drumkill' and they ungraciously called us 'black Knockenagh' because, I suppose, it needed a sharp eye to distinguish us from the shadows of the mountains. And we imagined a keen rivalry between us and them. But I realize now that there was no rivalry: the Drumkill people, if they thought of us at all, dismissed us as rustics.

When I was seven years old I began my education in the one-roomed building of Knockenagh Public Elementary School whose principal and entire staff was my father. The classroom was shabby and comfortless, its wooden floor treacherous with dry rot, its walls scabbed with a leprous damp, its two Gothic windows patched in places with balls of newspaper that had turned yellow with age. The twenty-odd pupils were arranged in four rows of long teak desks whose cast-iron supports were screwed to the floor. As I grew older I progressed back from the front row until, in my last couple of years, I proudly took my place with the big men and women along the rear wall.

In the beginning I remember being confused at the change

in my father's attitude to me once we were inside the class-room. At home I was 'Joe' or 'Joey boy' or even in his softer moments 'Plumb', a pet name from my baby days; but in school I was plain Hargan, just as Billy O'Brien was O'Brien and Máire O'Flaherty was O'Flaherty; and not only did I not get preferential treatment but an even stricter justice than the other pupils. And in the same way as I appeared to be two distinct persons to him, his son and his pupil, so he became two distinct persons to me: he was my father, kind, silent, troubled by an ambition I never understood until years later, and he was my teacher – the Sergeant, as he was nicknamed – stern, driving, humourless, rigid. As my schooling went on these two men, Father and the Sergeant, were so individual, each distinct in his own sphere, that never for a moment was I aware of an overlapping, not to talk of a fusion, of their identities.

Father came to Knockenagh in the summer of 1916 immediately after he left the teachers' training college in Dublin. It was a great honour for a young, untried man to be placed in charge of a school (and in those days there were over thirty on the roll) but he was worthy of it. He took first place in Ireland in his final examination; he was active and talented; and his contemporaries knew that Knockenagh was only a stepping stone to greater things and that as soon as Jack Hargan had a couple of years' experience behind him the clerical managers from all over the diocese would be vying with one another for him. He married and bought a house and when offers did come to him in those early years he turned them down because he was given an understanding (that is to say, a squeeze on the elbow and a knowing wink) by Father Carroll that as soon as the new school in Drumkill was built he would be the principal of it.

Ten years slipped away between the drawing up of the plans and the clearing of the site. We watched the town school rise from the ground and fill the shell of its scaffolding – snow-white walls, sheets of flashing windows, a roof of green, green tiles. And what we could not see we heard about on our Saturday evening visits to the town for Confession: that there were to be eight teachers, each with his own room; that each child was to have their own desk; and – crowning luxury for us who were served by one dry toilet whose stale odour lay heavy on our playground and in warm weather even permeated into the class-room itself – there were to be twenty-four flush toilets, twelve for boys and twelve for girls! I had the normal Knockenagh interest in this wonderful Drumkill creation but it was height-ened by the secret knowledge which burdened me like mortal sin and which I was forbidden to divulge to any of my friends: my father was to be the principal of this dazzling institution. How Mother fussed about the house those last weeks before the appointment was made, unable to restrain herself from making comments like 'It's scarcely worthwhile putting up fresh cur-tains' or 'One thing we'll all miss is the good healthy air up here'. And Father, although he never talked about his coming promo-tion, used to make excuses out to the front garden where he would stand gazing across at the shimmering building.

When he read in the local weekly paper that the appoint-ment had been given to a man from Armagh all he said was, 'It's gone,' and it was Mother, I remember, pious, docile Mother, who cried with anger and disappointment and spoke so unchar-itably about Father Carroll – now Monsignor Carroll – that she was troubled with scruples until she made her next Confession. As for me, I had mixed feelings. I was sad for Father because he had been hurt and sad too for myself because I was looking for-ward to escaping from the Sergeant's too personal interest in my progress. On the other hand I was now eleven years of age and it was generally accepted in the back row that Máire O'Flaherty and myself were as good as engaged and although we had never even held hands under the desk – not like O'Brien and Tessa McMahon – I had no wish to break up a betrothal so undemanding.

Even then Father should have left Knockenagh. He was only thirty-five years old when the town school opened. But he was too proud to reveal his pique by walking out immediately. He decided instead to hold on for a year and then look for a position outside the area altogether. But that did not happen either because his pride got another, severer blow which made the Sergeant even more rigid and my father more silent: the better-class Knockenagh families began sending their careful children into the Drumkill school. Besides reducing his meagre capitation grant this was a studied insult by his own people to his teaching ability. First the Martins asked for a transfer, then the O'Hagans, then O'Donnell's precious child, and in the end there were as many local children cycling into Drumkill each morning as straggled up to Knockenagh Public Elementary School.

Again Mother raged (and no doubt disturbed her soul a second time) and insisted that he lodge a complaint with Monsignor Carroll who was manager of both schools. This he did one Sunday morning after Mass. But the Monsignor, sibilant and abject in his apologies, explained that his hands were tied and that much as he himself would have preferred the parents to send their children to the school nearer to them he could not deny them their God-given right to choose the school they preferred.

On the following Monday morning the Sergeant, quiet and intense with determination, addressed his twelve bewildered pupils, telling them that he was going to make Knockenagh into the best school in the parish, the best school in the county, the best school in the country, whether they liked it or not, by God he was! Then, without further warning, he pointed a trembling finger at us four old-timers in the back.

'O'Brien, O'Flaherty, McMahon and you, Hargan, you four

are going to sit for the regional scholarship examination – and get it! Come on! Up to the front desk! Sharply!'

And for the next five weeks he drove us so relentlessly that, when he was stricken suddenly with pleurisy and the school had to be closed, two days of our new freedom had passed before our minds opened up again to thoughts of romance.

Monsignor Carroll claimed that Paul Desmond was an answer to prayer. It was not that substitute teachers were scarce – in those days there were more teachers than jobs for them – but most of the applicants became uncertain when they learned that the vacancy was in black Knockenagh and all of them declined the position when they saw the school they would have had to work in. The Monsignor was at his wits' end. He would gladly have turned the key in the door and forgotten about the place forever but he had Father on his hands and the twelve children of mulish parents who were insensitive to the attractions of single desks and flush toilets. Eventually, in puffing triumph, he arrived out at our house with Mr Desmond, the godsend.

'Saved, Jack! Saved! A knock at the door of the parochial house and out I goes and there is this young man who says to me, "I'm looking for temporary work as a teacher, Father. Have you anything to offer me?" Just like that! Straight from heaven!'

He dropped on to the edge of Father's bed and perspired with happiness.

'Can he teach?' Father asked.

'Can he teach? He's a graduate, Jack! Master of Arts, National University! Travelled! Cultured! A painter! Looking for something to tide him over before he goes off again on one of his – one of his sketching expeditions – something like that – But aren't we blessed, eh?'

'When can I see him?'

'Now, Jack! Right away! He's outside in the car!' The

Monsignor got to his feet and went to the door. 'By the way, how's the form?'

'Improving, Father.'

The Monsignor smiled confidently back at him as if to say that his pleas to heaven were obviously in a good run. Then he went pounding down the stairs to fetch the substitute.

Mr Desmond was boyish, tall, lanky, and fair. His movements were embarrassed, his manner hesitant. As Father's sharp eye assessed him he put his hands into the pockets of his jacket, then crossed them on his stomach, then held them behind his back.

'Have you seen the school?' Father asked defiantly. He was a little hard knot propped up – cornered almost – against the pillows.

'Yes, sir. Monsignor Carroll showed me over it. It is very – very compact –'

'We've toured all over the place, Jack,' the Monsignor broke in. 'Our last call was up with John Sharky to rent his cottage. And do you know what our young friend here tells me? – that Knockenagh reminds him of the countryside around Stuttgart! Can you beat that now!'

'And you are a National graduate?'

'Yes, sir.'

'So you can relax now, Jack, and get well at your leisure. Paul here will look after everything until you get back on your feet.'

'I have a special scholarship class this year, Mr Desmond –'

'Now, now, now, now, Jack, you'll never get well worrying like that. Leave everything in Paul's capable hands.'

'Are you a trained teacher?'

'No, sir. I – I just drifted around a bit after I graduated –'

'We'll disturb the patient no longer, Paul; he needs his rest. And if you have any difficulties Jack here will be only too pleased to help you out. Good. Then off we go and you can start tomorrow morning.' He caught Mr Desmond by the elbow and steered him to the door where I was standing, listening. 'Ah, the son and heir, isn't it?' he said, patting me on the head. 'Good boy. Good boy. Look after Daddy, won't you? Good men are scarce.'

Then he was gone and before he had turned his car at the gable of the house I was tearing across the fields to tell my friends that our liberty was at an end.

Since Father's illness I enjoyed a high prestige among the back-row set as the only source of authentic bulletins. During the critical period I was as happy as they were that the Sergeant might not pull through and I repeated the doctor's anxious doubts with genuine relish. Then the tide turned and we consoled ourselves with the knowledge that he would be laid up until Christmas at least and that even after that he would have to take things easy. Now that we were to have a new teacher the situation called for serious reappraisal.

'What's his name?' asked Billy O'Brien.

'Desmond.'

'Desmond what?'

'Just Desmond. Mr Desmond.'

'What'll he be like?' said Tessa McMahon.

'How would I know? All I know is that he is a painter.'

'He might paint the school,' said Máire, my betrothed.

'Not that kind of painter,' I explained. 'He's an artist painter.'

'We'll bloody-well paint *him* if he tries to get rough with us,' said Billy, spitting contemptuously. 'How's the Sergeant doing?'

'He got up for a while yesterday.'

'Trust him! I hope he slips and breaks his bloody neck.' Máire giggled. 'Is it true that he wears his long underpants in bed?'

'Billy says that he sleeps in his pelt,' Tessa joined in.

'He told this Desmond about us four being in a special scholarship class,' I said quickly, uneasy at their confusing of the private man with our teacher.

'And what did he say to that?' said Billy. 'Does he think he's

75

going to drive us through the exam? Because if he thinks that then he's really heading for trouble.'

'My da says that even if I get the scholarship he's not going to let me take it,' said Máire. 'He says I'm going to be a maid in the Melville Hotel in Drumkill.' And she tossed her ginger curls at me.

'You'll be no maid in the Melville,' said Billy. 'I'll tell you what you'll be – you'll be Mrs Hargan; you'll be Mr Plumb Hargan's maid!'

The girls howled with laughter and I blushed; Billy had the knack of implying a double meaning in the most simple remark.

'There'll be less old chat out of you tomorrow,' I said. 'This Desmond won't stand for any nonsense.'

'We'll see about that,' said Billy. 'If I'm any judge a week with us will be too much for him.'

Billy was no judge. Within three days Paul Desmond had charmed away our peasant reserve; within a week we were squabbling among ourselves over whose turn it was to light the fire or make his morning tea or carry his case up to the cottage he had rented at the top end of the townland. School became a new and astonishingly pleasant experience. We worked with potter's clay and raffia and wool and cane. We splashed hectic watercolours on to white sheets of paper, laughed uncertainly at our efforts, and began again in earnest. We read adventure stories about country children like ourselves who got caught up in mutiny and murder and civil war. We listened, still and solemn, to tales of life in Tangiers and Naples and Athens from the lips of the man who had actually witnessed the happenings he spoke of. And we sang – infants and all of us together – about Dixie and Avignon and Skye. Even the schoolroom itself changed. Our Gothic windows, we discovered, were made up of rich shades of blue and red and purple. On our walls we painted huge murals (one of Hannibal crossing the Alps, another of a Viking ship landing on our shore) in which the leprous patches were lost. And the desks, those massive teak desks, were unscrewed and, with all the thrill of desecration, moved into a semicircle around the teacher's desk.

But perhaps Paul Desmond's greatest miracle in us was our awakening to the countryside where we had spent all our days. For the first time in our lives we learned of the patterned behaviour of birds and thrust our faces into the heather to see a grasshopper crouch for a spring and watch a bowl of frogspawn turn to tadpoles and then to frogs. He brought us on nature rambles when we studied snipe and teal and grouse and woodcock. We climbed trees to peer cautiously into nests and waded in streams to catch caddis flies in jam jars. We fingered flowers, ordinary flowers whose heads we used to whack off with sticks, and learned how they came to be where they now grew and how they grew and all the magic of their pollination. In short he opened our eyes to the only wealth our dark, hillside home had to offer us in abundance and for that I have always remembered him with affection.

But the removal of drudgery from school life was for me merely a transfer. Each evening when I came home Father first questioned me endlessly and irritably on every half hour of Mr Desmond's tuition and then set me special lessons on reading, writing, and arithmetic, the three subjects his substitute was neglecting most, he felt. His bedroom became a second classroom. When my friends, I knew, were up in Mr Desmond's cottage, helping him to decorate it, or were gathered round him while he sketched the mountains behind him, there was I, seated on the edge of Father's bed, trying to learn the difference between the gerund and the gerundive, or battling with the cost of laying circular paths round gardens at so much per square foot. Occasionally Mother would join us – I was forbidden to take my eyes from my books but I could feel her standing behind me seconds before she spoke – to suggest in her mild way that perhaps a half hour's break would be good for both Father and me.

And to this Father would say, 'You want him to get this examination, don't you? You want him to achieve something, don't you? You don't want him to rot his life away here, do you?' Then, when she would have gone, he would say, as much to himself as to me, 'You will travel, son. You will travel and see that the far-off world is a beautiful place. And you will meet people with fine talk and fine manners. But you must be equipped first – Now, back to that problem –'

It was bedtime when he released me and only because Mother used to bribe me with sweets below in the kitchen could I bring myself in to say goodnight to him before I retired: it seemed so unnatural to kiss the Sergeant.

That autumn came to a slow end. We never saw the sun now and knew of its existence only from seeing it spotlight Drumkill for shortening hours each day. The first shafts of wild geese came in from the sea across the mountains and settled in the marshlands away to our right. The trees shed their leaves and retreated within themselves. There was no purring life in the heather.

Father was much better; a few more weeks and the doctor would allow him back to work. As his strength grew he concocted more and more difficult problems to torment my nights and weekends. As I became more sullen and more stupid his tongue became sharper and more hurtful. Máire had become cold and haughty towards me because of my neglect of her and now I really loved her. Her red hair sent my parsing astray and filled my blank maps with golden, curling rivers. And in school, my only pleasure, Mr Desmond taught us how to make masks of papier-mâché and wallpaper patterns with sliced potatoes.

It was the last Sunday of November and we were having our tea at the kitchen table when the Monsignor drew up at the front of the house and he and Frank O'Flaherty, Máire's father, barged in. The Monsignor's face was white and heavy, his lips massaging one another, his left eye winking rapidly half a dozen times in sly conspiracy. He stood in the doorway, blocking it with his broad frame, until he had signalled his anxiety to us; then he came into the kitchen, followed by O'Flaherty.

O'Flaherty was known locally as a thick man, easily offended, easily risen to anger, difficult to reason with. He was a rough, red-faced labourer who one day flogged his children brutally and the next led them with boisterous display into the town where he loaded them with sweets and ice cream and toys. I had always regarded him with caution because I felt that if he were to discover my love for his daughter he would exact a terrible vengeance from me.

'Well, well, well,' said the Monsignor. 'Eating, are we? Good. Carry on. Carry on. Don't let us interrupt you.'

'I'm on my way to the police,' O'Flaherty broke in. 'About that Desmond rip. By God, when I'm finished with him –'

'Now, Frank, calm, calm,' said the priest, staring hard at Father to show that this was the line that was to be followed with O'Flaherty. 'Easy, man. Easy. There's nothing to get excited about. Nothing at all.'

'What's the trouble, Monsignor?' said Father.

'Desmond! That's the trouble! It's easy for the priest here to say calm, calm, when it's not his child. But by God a man can't keep calm when a wastrel has pawed over his daughter! I'm going to the police! This very night!'

Máire, my Máire! And Mr Desmond!

'What has happened?' Father asked.

'Nothing, Jack. Nothing to speak of,' said the Monsignor. He made a pyramid of his chubby hands and spoke demurely down to it. 'Mr Desmond has – has been released from his position and I wanted to know if you are strong enough to resume –'

'I'll tell you what happened,' O'Flaherty said. 'He was kissing my wee girl! That's what happened! Billy O'Brien saw him!'

'O'Brien is only a child, Frank,' said the priest.

'He was there, wasn't he? He saw him, didn't he? For God's sake, he's not blind, is he?'

'When did this happen?' asked Father.

'This morning after first Mass,' said O'Flaherty. 'There were two or three of them up in the cottage with him as usual and he made a grab for our Máire and kissed her. On the mouth! The dirty old brute!'

'Could you take over again tomorrow, Jack?' The Monsignor's voice was so controlled that it was almost a whisper.

'Painting! Aye, that was a good lark! I said it to the missus. "He's no good, that fella," I said. "I wouldn't trust that fella as far as I would throw him!"'

'Where is he now?' said Father.

'He left on the afternoon train,' said the Monsignor. 'I saw him off myself.'

'You sacked him?'

'As soon as Frank here came to the parochial house to tell me what had happened I decided it was better –'

'You're damned right he sacked him and sneaked him out of the place before I got my hands on him! But he's not going to stop me going to the police. That fella's a menace and by God I'll put an end to his dirty tricks!'

'He's gone now, Frank,' said the priest. 'No harm done. No harm done.'

'What about Máire? Is she all right?' said Father, speaking my thoughts.

'I never asked her nothing,' said O'Flaherty. 'When I came home from last Mass and heard what had happened she felt the breadth of my belt across her, I can tell you. By God I taught her a lesson she'll not forget in a hurry!'

'Then Frank went to you, Monsignor, and you escorted Desmond to the train?' said Father.

'Yes. Yes,' said the priest, closing his eyes and nodding his head. 'He's in Dublin by now.'

'And I'm going to the police!' O'Flaherty shouted. 'If I had known you were going to sneak him out like that I would have dealt with him myself before I went to you. Am I right or am I not? Tell me that, Jack.'

'Did he say anything to you, Monsignor – when you accused him?'

'I accused him of nothing,' said the priest wearily. 'I just told him to pack his things and go.'

'Who was in the cottage at the time?' said Father, turning to O'Flaherty.

'There was young O'Brien and our Máire and one of the Tolands. And O'Brien saw him taking our Máire over to a couch in the corner and he had one hand on her neck and the other –'

'The child!' said Mother, indicating me. 'Not in front of the child!'

The Monsignor was alert again, grasping at the chance to change the conversation. 'And what about yourself, Jack? Are you well enough to turn out tomorrow?'

Father looked at Mother.

'I know it's not fair of me to ask you on such short notice,' the priest went on. 'But you understand how I am stuck. I am depending on you, Jack.'

'He's really not better yet, Monsignor,' said Mother.

'I know that, Mrs Hargan. But if he could possibly make it' – his jowls shook with sincerity – 'I would be forever in his debt. Well, Jack?'

'I will be in school tomorrow,' said Father.

'Good. Good. Now that's everything settled.' He turned to O'Flaherty. 'Are we ready for the road, Frank?'

'Are you going to drive me to the police station or do I walk it?' said O'Flaherty stubbornly.

'What's your advice, Jack? What do you think he should do?' Again the left eye fluttered and the lips rubbed together.

Father looked first at the Monsignor and then at O'Flaherty. At last he said, 'Do what the priest says, Frank. It's the best advice.' The Monsignor beamed gratitude back at him.

'I'll tell you what we'll do,' he said to O'Flaherty. 'We'll go into the town. Yes. And we will have a drink together in the parochial house. And we'll discuss the whole thing from alpha to omega. Right? Good. Good. That's settled then. A drink first in the parochial house.' He hustled O'Flaherty out before him and called back over his shoulder, 'I'll be out again tomorrow, Jack, to welcome you back to Knockenagh. And take things easy. Good men are scarce – very scarce.'

O'Flaherty still growled but the Monsignor kept on talking until he had him inside the car and then their voices were drowned by the roar of the engine.

The kitchen was silent again.

'God bless us and save us all!' said Mother. 'Young Mr Desmond! You never know anyone these days, do you?'

Father was not listening to her. 'An answer to prayer he called him that first day,' he said. 'Huh! But I wasn't fooled. I knew he was a fake the first moment I clapped eyes on him. And now the Monsignor knows that too – now when it's too late, as usual.'

'Are you sure you're well enough to go back?' said Mother anxiously.

'You heard him yourself, didn't you? Practically begged me.' He straightened his shoulders. 'I'll keep my word to him. I'll not let him down.'

Paul Desmond had stolen my girl! That was the last straw! I left the table before the meal was finished and fled to my room on the pretence of having lessons to do. There I flung myself across my bed and cried into the blankets until my ears hummed and my stomach hurt with heaving. I had nothing to live for anymore: I had no father but the Sergeant, and my mother now avoided my eyes in his presence, and when we were alone urged me to work harder and 'try not to upset him'. But worse, far worse than the loss of parents, I had lost, through my neglect of her, my Máire, my golden, laughing Máire, my sweet Máire. Every time I whispered her name to myself my stomach heaved again and tears filled my burning eyes and mercilessly I punished myself, saying her name over and over again, remembering her bright face and her freckled wrists and the quick, saucy movements of her head. And he, Desmond, had stolen her from me! Had tilted her face up to his and pressed his lips on hers! For all I knew had filled her ear with sunny tales of Venice and Malaga and Menton where they had planned to meet again in a week's time! The thief! The pig! The sneaking, smiling rotter! Slowly, deliberately, I cursed him to the blackest pits of hell.

But Máire – I saw her father's leather belt swing high in the air and come swishing down on her shoulders and back and arms and legs. And I closed my eyes and clenched my teeth and thrust myself between the strap and those delicate limbs and felt the searing pain bite into my own flesh. And then I saw her hold out her bare arms to me and the weals on them were raw and red and I kissed them tenderly and held them against my cheek and at the same time I spoke to her and soothed her with my love and told her that if she could forgive me for my carelessness in the past and smile at me again, just once, I would sit forever at her feet and be her slave and love her with all the urgent love in my heart.

She was late for school the following morning. We had unscrewed the teak desks and placed them back in their old position and had answered our names at roll call when the door opened and she breezed in, gay, fresh, her golden curls blown across her face by the wind. She was the prettiest sight I ever saw. My heart swelled up with nervous happiness.

She went up to the Sergeant at his desk to make her apology for being late, and while they talked together in low tones Billy O'Brien whispered across to me, 'Ask her about Desmond. You should have seen them courting away like hell on his couch! And her loving every minute of it!'

But I paid no attention to him because Máire was crying and showing her arms and hands to the Sergeant and he was looking at them and touching them gently with his finger tips and turning them over. Then, as I watched, he put his hand into his pocket and selected a coin and put it into her open palm. Her mouth said, 'Thank you, sir,' and she wiped away her tears and came down to her seat beside me.

Then was my time to speak to her. But I could not. Her presence beside me, the Sergeant's tender touching of her fingers and hands as I had seen myself touch them the previous night, his giving her money to atone for her father's brutality, the soft pushing of her side against my side, all sent my thoughts reeling so that the best I could manage was a choked, 'Hello, Máire.'

She looked at me and arched her eyebrows.

'Are you – are you all right?' I said.

'Look!' she said, her eyes dancing. 'My da bought it for me last night.' And she pulled open her cardigan to show me a gaudy gold necklace. 'Do you like it?'

'I love it,' I said with all the intensity of my being. Then, suddenly, it was time for milk break and we were out in the playground, O'Brien and Tessa McMahon and Máire and myself, in the sheltered corner near the road.

'Did you ask her?' said O'Brien.

'Ask her what?' I said guardedly.

'About Desmond.'

'Him!' said Máire pouting. 'If my da had got his hands on him he would have given him a fair trouncing!'

'What did the Sergeant say to you for being late?' Tessa asked.

'He gave me 2/6,' she said, and she smiled at me.

'God! He's gone off his rocker!' jeered Billy. 'He'll be looking for a court next!' He turned to Tessa. 'Wouldn't that be a sight to see, eh? The old Sergeant and Máire here wrestling on the couch!' The pair of them doubled up with laughing.

'That'll do you, O'Brien,' I said, my face flushed with anger, 'he's not a dirty pig like Desmond was.'

'But wouldn't it?' O'Brien went on, ignoring me. 'Can't you see him, Tessa, struggling away like blazes and his wee thin face all twisted up, trying to get a kiss! Oh, God, the Sergeant courting Máire!' I jumped on him. The first punch silenced him and the second sent him to the ground.

'He's my father, d'you hear! My father!' I roared. 'And if you say another word about him I'll hammer the head off you!'

Fortunately for me – because O'Brien was the best fighter in the school – the bell rang and Máire led me back to the classroom. But as I passed the teacher's desk he tapped me on the shoulder and said, 'I was watching you through the window. Why did you strike O'Brien?'

My false courage had now deserted me and I could not control the trembling of my lower lip.

'Well? I asked you a question. Why did you strike O'Brien?'

There was not a murmur in the room. Everyone was watching us, straining to catch what was being said.

'Because – because he called you the Sergeant!' I blurted out.

He gave me his handkerchief to wipe my eyes and said irritably in a voice that only I could hear, 'Go back to your seat, Plumb. Go back to your seat.'

Then, aloud and sharply, 'Open your arithmetics at page 27 – the area problems. Quickly! Quickly! Hurry up! Hurry up! We haven't all day. Get a move on! Starting at question number 4. Read it out, Hargan, please.' I began falteringly but by the time I came to the words 'How long would it take 5 men working 8 hours a day to do the same job?' with Máire beside me and my father in front of me, my tone was calm and relaxed and confident.

Foundry House

When his father and mother died Joe Brennan applied for their house, his old home, the gate lodge to Foundry House. He wrote direct to Mr Bernard (as Mr Hogan was known locally) pointing out that he was a radio-and-television mechanic in the Music Shop; that, although he had never worked for Mr Hogan, his father had been an employee in the foundry for over fifty years; and that he himself had been born and reared in the gate lodge. Rita, his wife, who was more practical than he, insisted that he mention their nine children and the fact that they were living in three rooms above a launderette.

'That should influence him,' she said. 'Aren't they supposed to be one of the best Catholic families in the North of Ireland?' So, against his wishes, he added a paragraph about his family and their inadequate accommodation and sent off his application. Two days later he received a reply from Mrs Hogan, written on mauve scented notepaper with fluted edges. Of course she remembered him, she said. He was the small, round-faced boy with the brown curls who used to play with her Declan. And to think that he now had nine babies of his own! Where did time go? He could collect the keys from the agent and move in as soon as he wished. There were no longer any duties attached to the position of gatekeeper, she added – not since wartime when the authorities had taken away the great iron gates that sealed the mouth of the avenue.

'Brown curls!' Rita squealed with delight when Joe read her the letter. 'Brown curls! She mustn't have seen you for twenty years or more!'

'That's all right, now,' was all Joe could say. He was moved with relief and an odd sense of humility at his unworthiness. 'That's all right. That's all right.'

They moved into their new house at the end of summer. It was a low-set, solid stone building with a steep roof and exaggerated eaves that gave it the appearance of a gnome's house in a fairytale. The main Derry-Belfast road ran parallel to the house, and on the other side the ground rose rapidly in a tangle of shrubs and wild rhododendron and decaying trees through which the avenue crawled up to Foundry House at the top of the hill. The residence was not visible from the road or from any part of the town; one could only guess at its location somewhere in the green patch that lay between the new housing estate and the brassiere factory. But Joe remembered from his childhood that if one stood at the door of Foundry House on a clear morning, before the smoke from the red-brick factories clouded the air, one could see through the trees and the under-growth, past the gate lodge and the busy main road, and right down to the river below from which the sun drew a million momentary flashes of light that danced and died in the vegetation.

For Joe, moving into the gate lodge was a homecoming; for Rita and the children, it was a changeover to a new life. There were many improvements to be made – there was no indoor toilet and no running water, the house was lit by gas only, and the windows, each made up of a score of small, diamond-shaped pieces of glass, gave little light – and Joe accepted that they were inevitable. But he found himself putting them off from day to day and from week to week. He did not have much time when he came home from work because the evenings were getting so short. Also, he had applied to the urban council for a money grant and they were sending along an architect soon. And he had to keep an eye on the children who looked on the grounds as their own private park and climbed trees and lit fires in the undergrowth and played their shrieking games of hide-and-seek or cowboys-and-Indians right up to the very front of the big house itself.

'Come back here! Come back!' Joe would call after them in an urgent undertone. 'Why can't you play down below near your own house? Get away down at once with you!'

'We want to play up here, Daddy,' some of them would plead. 'There are better hiding places up here.'

'The old man, he'll soon scatter you!' Joe would say. 'Or he'll put the big dog on you. God help you then!'

'But there is no old man. Only the old woman and the maid. And there is no dog, either.'

'No Mr Bernard? Huh! Just let him catch you and you'll know all about it. No Mr Bernard! The dog may be gone but Mr Bernard's not. Come on now! Play around your own door or else come into the house altogether.'

No Mr Bernard! Mr Bernard always had been, Joe thought to himself, and always would be – a large, stern-faced man with a long white beard and a heavy step and a walking stick, the same ever since he remembered him. And beside him the Great Dane who copied his master as best he could in expression and gait – a dour, sullen animal as big as a calf and as savage as a tiger according to the men in the foundry. And Mrs Hogan? He supposed she could be called an old woman now, too. Well over sixty, because Declan and he were of an age, and he was thirty-three himself. Yes, an old woman, or at least elderly, even though she was twenty years younger than her husband. And not Declan now, or even Master Declan, but Father Declan, a Jesuit. And then there was Claire, Miss Claire, the girl, younger than Declan by a year. Fat, blue-eyed Claire, who had blushed every time she passed the gate lodge because she knew some of the Brennans were sure to be peering out through the diamond windows. She had walked with her head to one side, as if she were listening for something, and used to trail her fingers along the boxwood that fringed both sides of the avenue. 'Such a lovely girl,' Joe's mother used to say. 'So simple and so sweet. Not like the things I see running about this town. There's something good before that child. Something very good.' And she was right. Miss Claire was now Sister Claire of the Annunciation Nuns and was out in Africa. Nor would she ever be home again. Never. Sister Claire and Father Declan – just the two of them, and both of them in religion, and the big house up above going to pieces, and no one to take over the foundry when the time would come. Everything they could want in the world, anything that money could buy, and they turned their backs on it all. Strange, Joe thought. Strange. But right, because they were the Hogans.

They were a month in the house and were seated at their tea, all eleven of them, when Mrs Hogan called on them. It was now October and there were no evenings to speak of; the rich, warm days ended abruptly in a dusk that was uneasy with cold breezes. Rita was relieved at the change in the weather because now the children, still unsure of the impenetrable dark and the nervous movements in the undergrowth, were content to finish their games when daylight failed, and she had no difficulty in gathering them for their evening meal. Joe answered the knock at the door.

'I'm so sorry to disturb you, Mr Brennan. But I wonder could you do me a favour?'

She was a tall, ungraceful woman, with a man's shoulders and a wasted body and long, thin feet. When she spoke her mouth and lips worked in excessive movement.

Rita was at Joe's elbow. 'Did you not ask the woman in?' she reproved him. 'Come on inside, Mrs Hogan.'

'I'm sorry,' Joe stammered. 'I thought – I was about to –' How could he say he didn't dare?

'Thank you all the same,' Mrs Hogan said. 'But I oughtn't to have left Bernard at all. What brought me down was this. Mary – our maid, you know – she tells me that you have a tape-recording machine. She says you're in that business. I wonder could we borrow it for an afternoon? Next Sunday?'

'Certainly, Mrs Hogan. Certainly,' said Rita. 'Take it with you now. We never use it. Do we, Joe?'

'If Sunday suits you I would like to have it then when Father Declan comes,' Mrs Hogan said. 'You see, my daughter, Claire, has sent us a tape-recording of her voice – these nuns nowadays, they're so modern – and we were hoping to have Father Declan with us when we play it. You know, a sort of family reunion, on Sunday.'

'Any time at all,' said Rita. 'Take it with you now. Go and get it, Joe, and carry it up.'

'No, no. Really. Sunday will do – Sunday afternoon. Besides, neither Bernard nor I know how to work the machine. We'll be depending on you to operate it for us, Mr Brennan.'

'And why wouldn't he?' said Rita. 'He does nothing on a Sunday afternoon, anyway. Certainly he will.'

Now that her request had been made and granted Mrs Hogan stood irresolutely between the white gaslight in the hall and the blackness outside. Her mouth and lips still worked, although no sound came.

'Sunday then,' she said at last. 'A reunion.'

'Sunday afternoon,' said Rita. 'I'll send him up as soon as he has his dinner in him.'

'Thank you,' said Mrs Hogan. 'Thank you.' Her mouth formed an O and she drew in her breath. But she snapped it shut again and turned and strode off up the avenue.

Rita closed the door and leaned against it. She doubled up with laughter. 'Lord, if you could only see your face!' she gasped between bursts.

'What do you mean, my face?'

'All scared-looking, like a child caught stealing!'

'What are you raving about?' he asked irritably.

'And she was as scared-looking as yourself.' She held her

hand to her side. 'She must have been looking for the brown curls and the round face! And not a word out of you! Like a big, scared dummy!'

'Shut up,' he mumbled gruffly. 'Shut up, will you?'

Joe had never been inside Foundry House, had never spoken to Mr Bernard, and had not seen Declan since his ordination. And now, as he stood before the hall door and the evil face on the leering knocker, the only introductory remark his mind would supply him was one from his childhood. 'My Daddy says here are the keys to the workshop and that he put out the fire in the office before he left.' He was still struggling to suppress this senseless memory when Father Declan opened the door.

'Ah, Joe, Joe, Joe! Come inside. Come inside. We are waiting for you. And you have the machine with you? Good man! Good man! Great! Great!'

Father Declan was fair and slight, and his gestures fluttering and birdlike. The black suit accentuated the whiteness of his hair and skin and hands.

'Straight ahead, Joe. First door to the right. You know – the breakfast room. They live there now, Father and Mother. Convenient to the kitchen, and all. And Mother tells me you are married and have a large family?'

'That's right, Father.'

'Good man! Good man! Marvellous, too. No, no, not that door, Joe, the next one. No, they don't use the drawing room anymore. Too large and too expensive to heat. That's it, yes. No, no, don't knock. Just go right in. That's it. Good man! Good man!'

One minute he was behind Joe, steering him through the hallway, and the next he had sped past him and was standing in the middle of the floor of the breakfast room, his glasses flashing, his arms extended in reception. 'Good man. Here we are. Joe Brennan, Mother, with the tape-recorder.'

'So kind of you, Joe,' said Mrs Hogan, emerging from behind the door. 'It's going to be quite a reunion, isn't it?'

'How many young Brennans are there?' asked Father Declan.

'Nine, Father.'

'Good! Good! Great! Great!'

'Such healthy children, too,' said Mrs Hogan. 'I've seen them playing on the avenue. And so – so healthy.'

'Have a seat, Joe. Just leave the recorder there. Anywhere at all. Good man. That's it. Fine!'

'You've had your lunch, Mr Brennan?'

'Yes, thanks, Mrs Hogan. Thank you all the same.'

'What I mean is, you didn't rush off without it?'

'Lucky for you, Joe,' the priest broke in. 'Because these people, I discover, live on snacks now. Milk and bananas – that sort of thing.'

'You'll find the room cold, I'm afraid, Mr Brennan.'

'If you have a power plug. I'll get this thing –'

'A power plug. A power plug. A power plug. A power plug.' The priest cracked his fingers each time he said the words and frowned in concentration.

'What about that thing there?' asked Mrs Hogan, pointing to the side of the mantelpiece.

'That's a gas bracket, Mother. No. Electric. Electric.' One white finger rested on his chin. 'An electric power plug. There must be one somewhere in the – ah! Here we are!' He dropped on his knees below the window and looked back exultantly over his shoulder. 'I just thought so. Here we are. I knew there must be one somewhere.'

'Did you find one?' asked Mrs Hogan.

'Yes, we did, didn't we, Joe? Will this do? Does your machine fit this?'

'That's grand, Father.'

'Good! Good! Then I'll go and bring Father down. He's in bed resting. Where is the tape, Mother?'

'Tape? Oh, the tape! Yes, there on the sideboard.'

'Fine! Fine! That's everything, then. Father and I will be down in a minute. Good! Good!'

'Logs,' said Mrs Hogan to herself. Then, remembering Joe, she said to him, 'We burn our own fuel. For economy.' She smiled bleakly at him and followed her son from the room.

Joe busied himself with rigging up the machine and putting the new tape in position. When he was working in someone's house it was part of his routine to examine the pictures and photographs around the walls, to open drawers and presses, to finger ornaments and bric-à-brac. But, here in Foundry House, a modesty, a shyness, a vague deference to something long ago did not allow his eyes even to roam from the work he was engaged in. Yet he was conscious of certain aspects of the room; the ceiling was high, perhaps as high as the roof of his own house, the fireplace was of black marble, the door handle was of cut glass, and the door itself did not close properly. Above his head was a print of horses galloping across open fields; the corner of the carpet was nibbled away. His work gave him assurance.

'There you are now, Mrs Hogan,' he said, when she returned with a big basket of logs. 'All you have to do is turn this knob and away she goes.'

She ignored his stiff movement to help her with her load of logs and knelt at the fireplace until she had built up the fire. Then, rubbing her hands down her skirt, she came and stood beside him.

'What was that, Mr Brennan?'

'I was saying that all you have to do is to turn this knob here to start it going and turn it back to stop it. Nothing at all to it.'

'Yes?' she said, thrusting her lips forward, her mind a blank.

'That's all,' said Joe. 'Right to start, left to stop. A child could work it.' He tugged at the lapels of his jacket to indicate that he was ready to leave.

'No difficulty at all,' she repeated dreamily. Then suddenly alert again, 'Here they come. You sit there, Mr Brennan, on this side of the fire, Father Declan will sit here, and I will sit beside the table. A real family circle.'

'You'll want to listen to this by yourselves, Mrs Hogan. So if you don't mind –'

'Don't leave, Mr Brennan. You will stay, won't you? You remember Claire, our lovely Claire. You remember her, don't you? She's out in Africa, you know, and she'll never be home again. Never. Not even for a death. You'll stay and hear her talking to us, won't you? Of course you will.' Her fingertips touched the tops of her ears. 'Claire's voice again. Talking to us. And you'll want to hear it too, won't you?'

Before he could answer the door burst open. Mr Bernard had come down.

It took them five minutes to get from the door to the leather armchair beside the fire, and Joe was reminded of a baby being taught to walk. Father Declan came in first, backward, crouching slightly, his eyes on his father's feet and his arms outstretched and beckoning. 'Slow-ly. Slow-ly,' he said in a hypnotist's voice. 'Slow-ly. Slow-ly.' Then his father appeared. First a stick, then a hand, an arm, the curve of his stomach, then the beard, yellow and untidy, then the whole man. Since his return to the gate lodge Joe had not thought of Mr Bernard beyond the fact that he was there. In his mind there was a twenty-year-old image that had never been adjusted, a picture which was so familiar to him that he had long since ceased to look at it. But this was not the image, this giant who had grown in height and swollen in girth instead of shrinking, this huge, monolithic figure that inched its way across the faded carpet, one mechanical step after the other, in response to a word from the black, weaving figure before him. Joe looked at his face, fleshy, trembling, coloured in dead purple and grey-black, and at the eyes, wide and staring and quick with the terror of stumbling or of falling or even of missing a syllable of the instructions from the priest. 'Lift again. Lift it. Lift it. Good. Good. Now down, down. And the right, up and up and up – yes – and now down.' The old man wore an overcoat streaked down the front with food stains, and the hands, one clutching the head of the stick, the other limp and lifeless by his side, were so big they had no contour. His breathing was a succession of rapid sighs.

Until the journey from door to armchair was completed Mrs Hogan made fussy jobs for herself and addressed herself to no one in particular. 'The leaves are terrible this year. Simply terrible. I must get a man to sweep them up and do something with the rockery, too, because it has got out of hand altogether –'

'Slow-ly. Slow-ly. Left. Left. That's it – up yet. Yes. And down again. Down.'

'I never saw such a year for leaves. And the worst of it is the wind just blows them straight up against the hall door. Only this morning I was saying to Mary we must make a pile of them and burn them before they smother us altogether. A bonfire – that's what we'll make.'

'Now turn. Turn. Turn. That's it. Right round. Round. Round. Now back. Good. Good.'

'Your children would enjoy a bonfire, wouldn't they, Mr Brennan? Such lively children they are too, and so healthy, so full of life. I see them, you know, from my bedroom window. Running all over the place. So lively and full of spirit.'

A crunch, a heavy thud, and Mr Bernard was seated, not upright but sideways over the arm of the chair, as he had dropped. His eyes blinked in relief at having missed disaster once more.

'Now,' said Mrs Hogan briskly, 'I think we're ready to begin, aren't we? This is Mr Brennan of the gate lodge, Daddy. He has given us the loan of his tape-recording machine and is going to work it for us. Isn't that kind of him?'

'How are you, Mr Hogan?' said Joe.

The old man did not answer, but looked across at him. Was it a sly, reproving look, Joe wondered, or was it the awkward angle of the old man's head that made it appear sly?

'Which of these knobs is it?' asked Father Declan, his fingers playing arpeggios over the recorder. ' "On". This is it, isn't it? Yes. This is it.'

'The second one is for volume, Father,' said Joe.

'Volume. Yes. I see. Well, all set?'

'Ready,' said Mrs Hogan.

'Ready, Daddy?' asked Father Declan.

'Daddy's ready,' said Mrs Hogan.

'Joe?'

'Ready,' said Joe, because that was what Mrs Hogan had said.

'Here goes then,' said Father Declan. 'Come in, Claire. We're waiting.'

The recorder purred. The soft sound of the revolving spools spread up and out until it was as heavy as the noise of distant seas. Mrs Hogan sat at the edge of her chair; Mr Bernard remained slumped as he had fallen. Father Declan stood poised as a ballet dancer before the fire. The spools gathered speed and the purring was a pounding of blood in the ears.

'It often takes a few seconds –' Joe began.

'Quiet!' snapped Mrs Hogan. 'Quiet, boy! Quiet!'

Then the voice came and all other sound died.

'Hello, Mammy and Daddy and Father Declan. This is Sister Claire speaking to the three of you from St Joseph's Mission, Kaluga, Northern Rhodesia. I hope you are all together when this is being played back because I am imagining you all sitting before a great big fire in the drawing room at this minute, Daddy spread out and taking his well-earned relaxation on one side, and you, Mammy, sitting on the other side, and Declan between you both. How are you all? I wish to talk to each of you in turn – to Declan first, then to you, Mammy, and last, but by no means least, to my dear Daddy. Later in the recording,

Reverend Mother, who is here beside me, will say a few words to you, and after that you will hear my school choir singing some Irish songs that I have taught them and some native songs that they have taught me. I hope you will enjoy them.'

Joe tried to remember the voice. Then he realized that he probably had never heard Claire speak. This sounded more like reading than speaking, he thought – like a teacher reading a story to a class of infants, making her voice go up and down in pretended interest.

She addressed the priest first and Joe looked at him – eyes closed, hands joined at the left shoulder, head to the side, feet crossed, his whole body limp and graceful as if in repose. She asked him for his prayers and thanked him for his letter last Christmas. She said that every day she got her children to pray both for him and for the success of his work and asked him to send her the collection of Irish melodies – a blue-backed book, she said, which he would find either in the piano stool or in the glass bookcase beside the drawing-room window.

'And now you, Mammy. You did not mention your lumbago in your last letter, so I take it you are not suffering so much from it. And I hope you have found a good maid at last because the house is much too big for you to manage all by yourself. There are many young girls around the mission here who would willingly give you a hand but then they arc too far away, aren't they? However, please God, you are now fixed up.'

She went on to ask about the gardens and the summer crop of flowers, and told of the garden she had beside the convent and of the flowers she was growing. While her daughter spoke to her Mrs Hogan worked her mouth and lips furiously and Joe wondered what she was saying to herself.

'And now I come to my own Daddy. How are you, Daddy? I am sure you were very sorry when Prince had to be shot, you had him so long. And then the Prince before that – how long did you have him? I was telling Sister Monica here about him the other day, about the first Prince, and when I said he lived to be nineteen-and-a-half she just laughed and said she was sure I was mistaken. But he *was* nineteen-and-a-half, wasn't he? You got him on my sixth birthday, I remember, and although I never saw the second Prince – you got him after I had entered – I am quite sure he was as lovely as the first. Now, why don't you get yourself a third, Daddy? He would be company for you when you go on your rambles and it would be nice for *you* to have him lying beside you on the office floor, the way the first Prince used to lie.'

Joe watched the old man. Mr Bernard could not move himself to face the recorder but his eyes were on it, the large, startled eyes of a horse.

'And now, Daddy, before I talk any more to you I am going to play a tune for you on my violin. I hope you like it. It is the "Gartan Mother's Lullaby". Do you remember it?'

She began to play. The music was tuneful but no more. The lean tinny notes found a weakness in the tape or in the machine, because when she played the higher part of the melody the only sound reproduced was a shrieking monotone. Joe sprang to his feet and worked at the controls but he could do nothing. The sound adjusted itself when she came to the initial melody again and he went back to his seat.

It was then, as he turned to go back to the fire, that he noticed the old man. He had moved somehow in his armchair and was facing the recorder, staring at it. His one good hand pressed down on the sides of his chair and his body rocked backward and forward. His expression, too, had changed. The dead purple of his cheeks was now a living scarlet, and the mouth was open. Then, even as Joe watched, he suddenly levered himself upright in the chair, his face pulsating with uncontrollable emotion, the veins in his neck dilating, the mouth shaping in preparation for speech. He leaned forward, half-pointing towards the recorder with one huge hand.

'*Claire!*'

The terrible cry – hoarse, breathy, almost lost in his asthmatic snortings – released Father Declan and Mrs Hogan from their concentration on the tape. They ran to him as he fell back into the chair.

Darkness had fallen by the time Joe left Foundry House. He had helped Father Declan to carry the old man upstairs to his bedroom and helped to undress him and put him to bed. He suggested a doctor but neither the priest nor Mrs Hogan answered him. Then he came downstairs alone and switched off the humming machine. He waited for almost an hour for the others to come down – he felt awkward about leaving without making some sort of farewell – but when neither of them came he tiptoed out through the hall and pulled the door after him. He left the recorder behind.

The kitchen at home was chaotic. The baby was in a zinc bath before the fire, three younger children were wrestling in their pyjamas, and the five elder were eating at the table. Rita, her hair in a turban and her sleeves rolled up, stood in the middle of the floor and shouted unheeded instructions above the din. Joe's arrival drew her temper to him.

'So you came home at last! Did you have a nice afternoon with your fancy friends?'

He picked his steps between the wrestlers and sat in the corner below the humming gas jet.

'I'm speaking to you! Are you deaf?'

'I heard you,' he said. 'Yes, I had a nice afternoon.'

She sat resolutely on the opposite side of the fireplace to show that she had done her share of the work; it was now his turn to give a hand.

'Well?' She took a cigarette from her apron pocket and lit it. The chaos around her was forgotten.

'Well, what?' he asked.

'You went up with the recorder, and what happened?'

'They were all there – the three of them.'

'Then what?'

'We played the tape through.'

'What's the house like inside?'

'It's very nice,' Joe said slowly. 'Very nice.'

She waited for him to continue. When he did not, she said, 'Did the grandeur up there frighten you, or what?'

'I was just thinking about them, that's all,' he said.

'The old man, what's he like?'

'Mr Bernard? Oh, Mr Bernard – he's the same as ever. Older, of course, but the same Mr Bernard.'

'And Father Declan?'

'A fine man. A fine priest. Yes, very fine.'

'Huh!' said Rita. 'It's not worth your while going out, for all the news you bring home.'

'The tape was lovely,' said Joe quickly. 'She spoke to all of them in turn – to Father Declan and then to her mother and then to Mr Bernard himself. And she played a tune on the violin for him, too.'

'Did they like it?'

'They loved it, loved it. It was a lovely recording.'

'Did she offer you anything?'

'Forced me to have tea with them, but I said no, I had to leave.'

'What room were they in?'

'The breakfast room. The drawing room was always draughty.'

'A nice room?'

'The breakfast room? Oh, lovely, lovely – Glass handle on the door and a beautiful carpet and beautiful pictures – everything. Just lovely.'

'So that's Foundry House,' said Rita, knowing that she was going to hear no gossipy details.

'That's Foundry House,' Joe echoed. 'The same as ever – no different.'

She put out her cigarette and stuck the butt behind her ear.

'They're a great family, Rita,' he said. 'A great, grand family.'

'So they are,' she said casually, stooping to lift the baby out of the bath. Its wet hands patterned her thin blouse. 'Here, Joe! A job for you. Dress this divil for bed.'

She set the baby on his knee and went to separate the wrestlers. Joe caught the child, closed his eyes, and rubbed his cheek against the infant's soft, damp skin. 'The same as ever,' he crooned into the child's ear. 'A great family. A grand family.'

The Illusionists

The annual visit of M L'Estrange to our school in the first week of March marked the end of winter and the beginning of spring. The bleak countryside around Beannafreaghan was cold-dead when he arrived and perhaps for a few weeks after he had gone, but when we heard the scrape of his handlebars against the school wall and saw his battered silk hat pass the classroom window the terrible boredom of winter suddenly seemed to vanish and we knew that good times were imminent.

We hadn't many visitors to Beannafreaghan Primary School where my father was principal and entire staff. Once a month Father Shiels, the manager, drove out the twisted five miles from the town, in one breath asked us were we good and told us to say our prayers, shook Father's hand firmly, and scuttled away again as if there were someone chasing him. Occasionally an inspector would come and Father would show him the seeping walls and the cracked windows and the rotting floor, and the inspector would grunt sympathetically and nod his head sadly from side to side and leave without asking us anything. An odd time a salesman for books would come but no one ever bought anything. And one morning a travelling theatre for schools, a great coloured caravan towed by a Land Rover, stopped at our gate and a man with a beard and an English accent breezed into the classroom. I distinctly overheard Father telling him that unfortunately it would be impossible to put on a play that day because the recording unit of the BBC was coming that very afternoon to make choral and verse-speaking tapes. The whole story, of course, was a fabrication: there wasn't a note or a line of verse in any of us. The truth of the matter was that his twenty-five pupils could not afford to pay sixpence a head, not to talk of two-and-six, not even to see an international cast doing international plays.

I never knew which I liked better: to be playing in the schoolyard at lunchtime, and look up, and suddenly see the tall figure of M L'Estrange mounted on his bicycle and free-wheeling recklessly down the long hill that hid us from the town of Omagh; or to be in class, staring dreamily at an open book, and then to hear the scrape of his handlebars against the school wall. I think I preferred him to walk in on us when we were in the middle of lessons, to see the door opening, to hear his deep, resonant voice boom out, 'Am I interrupting the pro-gress of knowledge?' because then the delight was so acute that the mouth dropped open, and the eyes stared, and the heart raced, because there he was, M L'Estrange, The Illusionist, back again to perform his magic for us. To us rustic children he was the most wonderful man in the world.

Father was stiffly polite to the manager and over-anxious with inspectors but he welcomed M L'Estrange warmly and enthusiastically. Mother's attitude to the illusionist was at least consistent – she treated him quietly and with caution. But I could never understand Father's attitude. There was no doubt that he was delighted to see him. He put his arm round his shoulder and pumped his hand, and kept looking at us to find a match for his heartiness in our faces (perhaps he mistook our stillness for indifference). But, as the afternoon went on, his exuberance quickly evaporated, and he became irritable again, and by the time M L'Estrange left our house to cycle back to town – always late in the evening, and by then Father and he were more than half drunk – Father had begun taunting him about being nothing more than a trick-of-the-loop man and scarcely better than a tramp. But when he first arrived you would think Father had found a long-lost brother. He would exclaim, 'Look, children! Look who's here! M L'Estrange! Back again!' As if there was any need to tell us to look. Because the moment he appeared in the doorway our quick, country eyes devoured him: the calm face; and the slender white hands; and the long silvery hair that had given a gloss to the collar of his frock coat; and the black striped trousers, frayed at the bottom; and the soiled white scarf; and the glittering rings. And then, long before I had finished gazing at him, Father would send me across the fields to the house to tell Mother to have a meal ready for M L'Estrange after the performance. That was a job I hated doing. Mother never shared my excitement – 'Don't tell me that old trickster's here again!' – and by the time I got back the show was ready to begin. It was little consolation to me that, later in the evening when all the other pupils had dispersed, I would have M L'Estrange all to myself in my own house. What mattered was that invariably I missed the preparations: the clearing of Father's table; M L'Estrange putting on his black mask; the hanging of the curtain between the blackboard and the fireplace; the arranging of the desks in three rows. The smallest children, frozen with delicious nervousness, sat in the front seats, the bigger ones sat in the middle, and the biggest along the back. Father stood at the door and smoked, his face relaxed and smooth with content.

Then M L'Estrange would begin. He would stand in front of us for a few minutes, his hands joined at his chest as if he were praying, his lean, lined face raised and immobile, and stare at us with those soft, sad eyes of his. Mesmerized, we stared back at him, our throats drying with anticipation, giggles stirring and promptly dying in our stomachs. Suddenly he would crack his fingers and say 'Would someone please open a window at the back of the auditorium?' or 'Would it be possible to have a spot-light switched on?' in a voice so unexpectedly quiet and persuasive that instinctively we all moved to do his bidding, so great was our relief that he had spoken, so hypnotic was his power over us. From then on he had us in the palm of his hand.

Although I saw his tricks every year for five or six years I remember only two of them. In one he knotted a heavy rope to a back tooth, gave the rope a tug, and out came a heavy wooden molar, the size of a turnip. The other trick I remember was with a rabbit who had dull, weary eyes like Mother's. He sat the rabbit on Father's table, surrounded it with four sheets of cardboard, covered it with a black cloth, and to our horror collapsed the box with a great thump of his fists. Of course the rabbit had disappeared. With a tired smile he produced it from under his jacket.

We knew the show was over when M L'Estrange walked over to where Father stood and led him by the hand to the middle of the classroom. Together they stood before us, both of them smiling and bowing (I was always embarrassed at Father bowing, as if he had been part of the entertainment) while we clapped and cheered and whistled and stamped our feet. Then Father made a speech of appreciation, thanked M L'Estrange for 'including humble Beannafreaghan in his overcrowded itinerary', reminded us to bring twopence each the next day – he paid the illusionist out of his own pocket, and during the following weeks badgered and cajoled his pupils to reimburse him – and gave us the rest of the afternoon off. It was then that I knew one of the few advantages of being the teacher's son: every year I was privileged to wheel M L'Estrange's bicycle, with its precious box that held the rabbit and the giant tooth and the other sacred things securely sealed in a box attached to the carrier, from the school to our house. It was a quarter of a mile by road, and I was accompanied by a retinue of a dozen or more amateur illusionists who pantomimed around me, yanking out their teeth, and producing rabbits from school-bags, and who offered me all the wealth of their pockets if I would allow them even to touch the rim of the mudguard.

M L'Estrange's last visit to Beannafreaghan in the March of my tenth year is the one I remember most vividly because I had spent the whole doleful winter waiting for it. Father had decided that I was to be sent to a Jesuit boarding school in Dublin the following September (like so many of his grand plans this one fell through, too; when September came Mother got the Christian Brothers in the town to take me in as a day pupil) and I had made up my mind that I would escape that terrible fate by getting M L'Estrange, when he would come, to take me away with him as an apprentice illusionist. I knew that a busy man like him could do with an assistant who would organize his tours, and see to advance bookings, and look after his accoutrements. My plans were not altogether impracticable: I had a small bicycle of my own; and from my mentor I would learn his craft so that when he would retire I would become a professional illusionist myself. Throughout the year I had put all my pocket money into a cocoa tin so that when my apprenticeship would begin I would have a measure of financial independence. I told no one of my scheme. And that March, as I wheeled M L'Estrange's bicycle from the school to the house, I remember watching the others clowning around me and thinking how young and silly they were. Little did they know the wonderful future that was before me.

Father and M L'Estrange sauntered in about half-an-hour later. As Father's good humour unaccountably dwindled the illusionist's increased. He bowed theatrically to Mother and addressed her as Madame, and I believe he would have raised her hand to his lips had she not pulled it away and said in her flattest Tyrone accent, 'I suppose you're famished as usual, Mister, are you?'

'I'll not say no to a morsel, Madame,' said the illusionist with a roguish smile. 'I'll not say no.'

And for a man with such white hands and such a lean, patient face he had a huge appetite. Indeed so hungrily did he eat that Father did all the talking and M L'Estrange only grunted 'I see' or 'Yes' or 'Imagine' between mouthfuls. When the meal was

over Father produced a bottle of whiskey, pulled two chairs up
to the range, and the illusionist and himself sat talking and
drinking at the fireside, as they did every year, until night came
down on Beannafreaghan and the whiskey was done.

That winter had been particularly severe. There was still
snow on the hilltops and the fields were rigid with black frost
when M L'Estrange came. We hadn't heard a bird in five months.
Had I not had the evidence of the illusionist sitting in our kitchen and chatting to my father I would not have believed that
spring was at hand. Their talk followed the usual pattern. At
first they spoke of the satisfaction to be got from teaching
school in a small rural community, 'striking a spark that could
cause a conflagration', as the illusionist called it, and from travelling around the countryside, 'opening the ready hearts of
children to laughter', as Father called it. They agreed that each
vocation had its unique rewards. Then they talked about the
changes they had witnessed over the years: only really dedi-
cated teachers now taught in decaying, shrinking schools; and
only really altruistic troupers still entertained their pupils.
Then they went away back to the past, and from there on it
wasn't really a conversation at all, but two monologues spoken
simultaneously, each man remembering and speaking his memories aloud. And eventually, when the bottle was empty, Father
became sarcastic.

Mother refused to be drawn into their talk. M L'Estrange
would try to engage her, but she shook him off quickly. 'You're
nothing but a pair of blatherskites!' Throughout the whole
afternoon and evening she never stopped working, baking
bread, washing clothes in the zinc bath, boiling nettles for the
hens, scalding the milking tins, chopping vegetables for dinner
the next day, all the time bustling about the kitchen so that she
was constantly coming between me and the two men, and
making so much noise with her buckets and basins that I missed
a lot of what was being said. Not that I minded missing Father's

reminiscences – I had heard them so often that I knew them backways – but now that I was on the brink of a new life every word that M L'Estrange had to say about his early career was of the utmost interest. But worse than the din she made she tried to make conversation with me – 'Have you no exercise to do?' 'Any fun at school today?' 'Why don't you go out for a run on your bicycle?' 'Are you not taking the dog out for a walk?' – and when I answered her in sharp monosyllables she invented jobs for me to do: feed the calf; bring in sticks; get water from the well; close the meadow gate. The result was that I heard only part of the monologues and witnessed only the last half of the row when M L'Estrange called Father a soured old failure and Father called M L'Estrange a down-at-heel fake and warned him never to set foot in Beannafreaghan again.

'The summer I qualified,' Father was saying into his glass as I spread the sticks for the morning fire along the front of the range, 'I came first place in the whole of Ireland. And there wasn't a manager in the thirty-two counties who wouldn't have given his right arm for me. His right arm, Sir.'

'France is the country,' said M L'Estrange, turning his rings idly. 'That's where they had appreciation. A hundred thousand francs for an hour's performance. *La Belle France*.'

'Dublin – Cork – Galway – crying out for me. An old PP drove up the whole way from Kerry, three-hundred-and-fifty miles, to ask me personally to take over a school in Killarney. "We would be honoured to have you, Mr Boyle," he said.'

'Ah, the drawing rooms of London in the early Twenties! Lords and ladies and all the quality of the land. Lloyd George once shook my hand and said it was a pleasure to see me perform.'

'But would I go? Oh, no! Beannafreaghan, I said. That's the place for me. Beannafreaghan. Because Beannafreaghan needed a teacher that had something more to give, just that little bit more than the other fellow.'

'A pleasure to see me perform. The year 1920. In London-derry House, London, capital of the world.'

'I'm telling you, if I hadn't taken up the challenge that summer, bloody Beannafreaghan Primary School would have been closed down and all the bloody children would have grown up illiterate.'

'Top of the bill in Leeds and Manchester and Glasgow and Brighton.'

'Bloody illiterates and too bloody good for them.'

'M L'Estrange, Prince of the Occult.'

'Fifteen years ago the Very Reverend John Shiels, PP, came out to me here, and stood in this very kitchen, and asked me – bloody-well begged me – to take over the new school in the town. Wasn't another man in the whole of County Tyrone competent to tackle it.'

'I drove my own car, and stayed in the best hotels, and picked and chose the engagements I wanted. There was respect for illusionists in those days, respect and admiration.'

'And what, said I straight out to him, and what would happen to Beannafreaghan?'

'I saw me ordering swank dinners for the whole cast and tipping the waiters with pound notes.'

'That never occurred to him. Oh, no! But it occurred to me. They may be country children, I said to him, and they may not have the most modern school building, but by God they deserve the best teacher in the country, top of my class the summer I qualified, and they're bloody-well going to have the best teacher in the country! I'm not going to desert them, I said to him.'

'My Lords, Ladies, and Gentlemen, things are not what they appear. The quickness of the hand deceives the eye. I was entrusted with the secret of this next act by the Sultan of Mysore –'

'And I didn't desert them. I'm bloody-well still here, amn't I? In spite of all the offers I got. Hundreds of them. Only fifteen years ago in this very kitchen –'

'In his white marble palace in the hills where the sun shines all day –'

'I'm still here! The proof of the pudding is in the eating!'

'It's all in the mind. The powers of the mind are beyond our comprehension.'

At that stage Mother ordered me out to the byre with her to milk the cow. I held the hurricane lamp while she milked. She could do the job in five minutes when she wished but that night she seemed to take hours at it. 'Hurry up! Hurry up!' I kept saying because I was afraid that M L'Estrange would have gone before we got back to the house.

'What do you want to be listening to the ravings of two drunk men for?' she said. 'I don't know what takes that trickster here anyway, upsetting everybody.' And she rested her forehead against the red cow's side and pulled the teats as if she never wanted the milking to end.

While we were out the row began. In the still, frosty night we heard their angry voices as we turned the gable of the byre. Their talk always ended with Father taunting the illusionist. But never until that night had M L'Estrange answered him back; he just lifted his hat from behind the kitchen door and went off without a word into the darkness. But that year, when my whole future depended on him, he had to lose his temper.

'My God!' said Mother. 'They'll kill each other.' And the pair of us ran up to the house.

M L'Estrange was on the street, and Father was standing in the doorway, and they were shouting at each other. Father held on to the doorposts for support, and the illusionist swayed back and forward and pointed an accusing finger at him. They were both ugly with hate.

'Go home to your hovel, wherever it is!' Father roared. 'Bloody tramp!'

'Beannafreaghan is the place for you!' M L'Estrange called back. 'The back end of nowhere!'

'And where did you pick up the name L'Estrange, eh? I know who you are, Monsieur Illusionist L'Estrange: your real name's Barney O'Reilly, and you were whelped and bred in a thatched cottage in County Galway!'

'They wouldn't give you a job in the town if there wasn't another teacher in the whole country!'

'You were never in London or Paris in your life! And your wee cheap tricks wouldn't fool a blind jennet!'

'You're stuck here till the day you die!'

'Mister Barney O'Reilly – fake!'

'A soured old failure!'

'Never put a foot in Beannafreaghan again or we'll set the dogs on you!'

'Don't you worry, Boyle. You'll never see me again.'

Mother sprang between them. She pushed Father into the hallway and then wheeled on the illusionist.

'Get out of this place!' she spat at him with a fierceness I never saw in her before. 'Get away out of here and never darken the door again, you – you – you sham, you fake, you!'

Then she saw me standing with the hurricane lamp in my hand.

'Get inside at once!' she snapped. 'You should have been asleep hours ago.'

I did not dare disobey her, so mad was she. As I passed her on my way into the house she shoved me roughly in the back and bolted the door behind me.

Father was standing uncertainly in the middle of the kitchen floor. He tried to look defiantly at her.

'I told him a thing or two that he needed to –' he began.

'Get off to your bed,' said Mother sharply. 'And shame on you making a scene like that before the child.'

'I told him a few home truths. I let him know what I thought of –'

'Shut up! Hasn't there been enough said for one night? Go and get some sleep, or you won't be fit to go to work tomorrow.'

As he lurched towards the door he tried to wink at me but his two eyes closed.

'He forgot his beautiful hat!' he said, sniggering, lifting the shabby topper down from behind the door.

'Run after him with it,' said Mother to me. 'I don't want him coming back to look for it. Run, child, run.'

That should have been my opportunity. Confused and frightened as I was with the shouting and the hate and the sickening sight of Father and M L'Estrange abusing each other, a part of my mind was still lucid, still urged me: Now, now, now. I saw the cocoa tin on the mantelpiece; I knew my bicycle, polished, oiled, pumped, was in the turf shed; I thought of the Dublin boarding school. But suddenly the dream that I had nursed all winter lost its urgency, required an effort and determination I couldn't muster. If by some miracle Mother were to say, 'Go off with M L'Estrange, son. Travel the world with him,' or if M L'Estrange were to come back and say in his persuasive voice, 'Your son and I have planned to make a grand tour of Ireland and England and the whole of Europe,' then I would have floated off with him, and together we would have drifted happily from theatre to theatre, from country to country. But now I stood trembling, numbed, petrified with irresolution.

'Will you hurry up! He won't have got the length of the school yet,' said Mother.

I unbolted the door and ran out into the hushed night.

I found M L'Estrange on his hands and knees on the road below the byre. He was crawling towards his bicycle which lay spinning five yards beyond him. He smiled drunkenly up at me.

'It would appear, my friend, that my trusty steed and I parted company.'

The moonlight gave his face the pallor of a corpse. His long, thin fingers were spread out before him like the witch's in *Hansel and Gretel*.

'You forgot your hat.'

'Would you be kind enough to lift my bicycle for me? Once I get up on it nothing can stop me. The problem is –' He hiccoughed and mumbled, 'Excuse me – The problem is to get mounted, if you understand what I mean.'

I left the hat within his reach and went to lift the bicycle.

Before I got it I found the giant tooth lying on the road. Beside it was the square of black cloth. Further on I found the four sheets of cardboard, and the mask, and a packet of balloons. I picked them up and carried them to the bicycle. It was then that I saw that the box on the carrier was open and empty. The rabbit! The rabbit had escaped! I was about to shout, to cry out to M L'Estrange that his rabbit was gone when I saw it crouching beside the front wheel. Silently, cautiously, I tiptoed over to it. But there was no need for silence or caution: it never moved. I gathered it gently in my arms and looked into its face. Its dull, weary eyes, Mother's eyes, stared back at me, beyond me. Had its heart not tapped against my fingertips I might have thought it was dead. I put it in the box on top of the black cloth and closed the lid.

M L'Estrange was at my side.

'All set?' he said. 'Once more into the breach, dear friends, once more.'

He was wearing the top hat now and it sat jauntily on the side of his head.

'As I say,' he went on, 'once I get mounted nothing can stop me, nothing in the wide world.' He put an arm on my shoulder to steady himself. 'As for you, my good friend, accept this little token from M L'Estrange, Prince of the Occult.'

He slipped a coin into my hand. Then he gripped the handlebars, held the bicycle away from him, and said in his resonant voice that carried over the still, dead countryside, '*Au revoir!*'

Then he moved off. He looked back at me to see was I watching him (I think he was going to attempt to get up on the

bicycle). But when he saw me looking after him he waved to me
and went on walking. A bend in the road hid him from me.

In the light of the kitchen I saw that he had given me a penny.
I dropped it into the cocoa tin. Father was in bed and Mother
was spooning my night porridge into a bowl.

'He's away, is he?' she asked.

I said he was.

'Sit down and take your supper,' she said. 'You're famished
with the cold.'

'He gave me half-a-crown!' I blurted it out because I thought
I was going to cry.

'Aye?' she said, giving me a shrewd look.

'And he said that he'll come to see me in the boarding school
in Dublin.' I couldn't stop myself now. 'And he said that when
I'm a big man he'll take me away with him and teach me all his
magic and we'll go to France and Germany and Spain and India
and we'll see the seven seas and visit great palaces and carry
red-and-gold parrots on our shoulders and drive about in big
cars and stay in grand hotels and – and – and –'

Then the tears came, pouring out of me, and Mother's arms
went round me, and I buried my face in her breast, and sobbed
my heart out.

'And – and he was so drunk he fell off his bicycle and he
could hardly walk. And only for me he would have lost his
rabbit and his giant tooth and –'

'There, there, there,' said Mother, rocking me against her
and stroking the back of my head. 'It's all over now. It's all over.
All over. It'll be forgotten in the morning. And, before we
know where we are, spring will be here, and you'll be away in
Tracey's lorry to the bog to cut turf, and the birds will come
back and begin nesting –'

'I told you a lie – it was a penny he gave me!'

'– and we'll bring the skep of bees up to the mountain for the
heather,' she went on, as if she hadn't heard me. 'And we'll

whitewash the byre until it sparkles – remember the fun we had last year? – and before we know it will be summer, and we'll take the rug down to the meadow, and lie in the shade of the chestnut tree, and listen to the cow eating the clover, and we'll take a packet of biscuits with us and a can of buttermilk, and we'll have a competition to see who can drink it the quickest – remember last year? – and on the hottest day of summer – oh, it'll be so hot it will kill us to laugh! – we'll empty the well and climb down into it in our bare feet, and scrub it out, and yo-ho to each other down there – remember? remember? – and we'll laugh until we're weak, and oh my God, oh the great fun we'll have – oh dear God it'll be powerful – when the good weather comes.'

I stopped crying and smiled into her breast because every word she said was true. But it wasn't because I remembered that it was true that I believed her, but because she believed it herself, and because her certainty convinced me.

Ginger Hero

At the time I'm thinking about, the year Billy Brogan and I bought our own fighting cock and matched him against the best birds in Ireland, you would never have suspected that Annie and Min were sisters. Ten years earlier, when Billy married Annie and I married Min, they were as like as two peas, although, strangely enough, it was Min who was the softer of the two then. But they had changed so much in the decade that you would have been hard put to find any resemblances between them. Annie had grown into a big, fat hearty woman who spent her days – except when she went to the cockfights with Billy and me – in a wicker chair in front of the open hearth, her legs wide apart and an all-enveloping apron stretched across them, her chubby hands lying limp on her lap, and her gentle eyes waiting for half an excuse to stream with laughter. Maybe the house could have been tidier – there was nobody but Billy and herself to upset it, and Billy was as natty as an old maid – but she never seemed to notice it.

'Look at the state of the place!' she would say, struggling to her feet when you would go in. 'You would think I had a houseful of children!' And she would burst into such an infectious laugh that you forgot about the bucket of soiled clothes at the door and the breakfast dishes still on the table and the crumbs on the floor, and laughed with her. And although it was Billy who cleared a seat for you and wiped it clean with his hand it was Annie who made you feel at home.

Not that our house was much tidier. But then we had eight children and even if Min slaved from morning to night, as she did, there was always a toy somewhere to trip you or a row of steaming nappies to hide the fire from you. Poor Min, those first ten years were sore on her, made her thin and haggard and harrassed-looking. When I would see herself and Annie together I would wonder at how time had sharpened the one and mellowed the other: my wife with all the worries in the world and a wrinkle to show for every one; Billy's wife apparently without a care. I often thought that if he had not had such an obsession about being childless he could have been the happiest man in Donegal.

He was a strange buck, Billy. We were brothers-in-law; we worked together on Lord Downside's estate (Billy was land steward, in charge of twenty of us); we spent most of our weekends together; but for all that you never knew what he was thinking. He had been an amateur bantamweight boxer in his single days and had never lost his pride in his physique. He was small and muscular and intense, without a superfluous ounce of flesh. His hair and eyebrows were sandy and his eyelashes so long that, when his eyes were closed, they touched the two tufts of bright ginger hair that sprouted from the top of his high cheekbones. When you were talking to him he had the habit of tilting up that protruding chin of his, and closing his mouth in a sort of humourless grin, and hiding his eyes behind those silken lashes, and you could never tell whether he was listening to you or not. And yet, in spite of his remoteness and his quick temper and his passion for having everything correct, I always liked Billy.

The workmen of the estate admired him but they never warmed to him. They were jealous of the way he kept himself, of his careful appearance, of his measure of prosperity. They were all struggling on a meagre wage, just as I was myself, and although Billy could not have had more than a couple of pounds a week more than ourselves, he had only Annie and himself to support, and his pay packet was well able for that. The rest of us had armfuls of children to keep. In the early years of his marriage they would rag him about a family, and in the beginning he gave back as good as he got. But as time went on and there was still no sign of a child they stopped joking to his face because he would go very still and his eyelashes would flicker. Behind his back, of course, they had many a good laugh about him: they wondered did The Bantam, as they called him, lead a married life at all; they wondered had his boxing career impaired him in some inexplicable way; they proposed all sorts of cures – from putting him on a diet of goat's milk to calling on Annie themselves. Then, when they made ribald jokes about Annie, I would tell them to shut up, not because she was my sister-in-law, but from a sense of loyalty to Billy; and maybe, too, because she reminded me so much of the Min I had married.

There was a row in our house every Sunday Billy and I went to a cockfight.

'Traipsing about like tinkers, and gambling behind wee hills, and mixing with all the good-for-nothings in the country, and running from the police!' Min would snap at me. 'It's all very well for Billy Brogan that has neither chick nor child. But you – you have responsibilities, if you only knew it!' And when Annie began travelling around in the van with us she went mad altogether. 'Oh, aye! Go ahead and enjoy yourselves! Leave me here to wrestle with your children! Go ahead and have your fun! Since the day I married you what have I ever been but a housekeeper and a nursemaid! Go on! Go on! Gamble your few shillings away!'

These tirades were for my ears alone. When Billy would call for me she would be as sweet as could be. 'So you're off for a bit of fun, Billy? Well, why wouldn't you? It's going to be a nice afternoon. Take care of yourselves now, and good luck!' Whatever it was about him she had a powerful respect for him. I often thought, watching her looking at him in his neat Sunday suit and his immaculate shirt and his shining shoes, that she was not at all sure her sister had not got the better man. And out in the van, with Annie wedged between him and me, and seeing her look up so honestly into that fair, uncommunicative face of his, I knew that she had no doubts at all.

Billy was an expert on cocks. I had never seen a fight until he brought me to one, three or four years after we had married; and, although he had become interested in the sport only a year before I did, he had made a study of every detail of it, just as he had studied crop rotation and pig breeding and Ayrshire cows. So when Spittles Sheridan sent word to me that he had a promising year-old bird for sale I could not wait to tell Billy.

'All he wants is ten pounds,' I said. 'It's for nothing, man! A gift! You know yourself that his birds have the best of stuff in them.'

His mouth was shut tight and his eyelashes slept on his cheeks.

'Look, Billy,' I went on, 'this is our chance. We'll never make money betting on strange birds. But with a bird of our own, trained by us, we could make a wee fortune. Five pounds each is all that it will cost us. We'll make that much – three times that – on the first time it's out. What do you say?'

'I'll think about it,' he said, without opening his eyes.

'Think be damned! There's no time to think about it. If we don't take it before the weekend Tony McGrenra or Hoppy Reilly or McHugh from Frosses will have grabbed it.'

'Colour?'

'Ginger. And Spittles claims –'

'Age?'

'Twelve months.'

'You're sure he has never set it?'

'He swears he hasn't.'

'Weight?'

'For God's sake, man, I haven't seen the thing myself yet!'

He opened his eyes then and smiled slowly at me.

'You're interested or you're not — which is it?' I said sharply, because his calmness always angered me when I was enthusiastic.

'I'll tell you what, Tom,' he said. 'We'll go and have a look at it on Saturday. Satisfied?'

I was not satisfied but I knew I would wait.

'I hope we're not too late then, that's all.'

'We won't be,' he said. 'Don't let that worry you. We won't be.'

He was right, of course: the bird was still there. I was disappointed in it. I thought its legs should have been longer and I did not like the easy way it carried itself. I expected a mature cock with fiery eyes and jerky steps and lightning movements of the head and neck, but this bird was thin and undeveloped and domesticated.

Spittles stood behind us.

'It's nothing but a broody hen, that,' I whispered to Billy who was crouched on the floor of the byre. 'Come on away home.'

He held it in his hands — it sat there, patient, docile — and under the ginger feathers and over the white transparent flesh his gentle fingers explored the breast and the back and the long neck, kneading, pressing, massaging, caressing slowly and with assurance, until the bird's eyes became drunken and its head rose and fell like an old man dozing before a fire.

'It's a bloody chicken,' I said into his ear. 'It couldn't beat its way out of a wet paper bag! It wouldn't last five seconds against a good crow!'

He did not hear me. The bird was sotted now and spread its toes in an ecstasy of pleasure. But still he worked at it, rubbing its thighs between fingers and thumb.

'Billy!' I hissed. 'That thing will never be a cock!'

'What?' he said, aware of me for the first time.

'Are you coming home?'

He put the bird carefully on the ground, watched it stagger, shake itself, and walk away; then he got to his feet. Spittles came between us, his chin wet as usual with saliva.

'Yes, boys? A great bird, eh? One hell of a fine bird, eh?'

'He'll make a good mattress,' I said. 'After some sparrow kills him with one peck.'

'Ah, now Tom —'

'Seven pounds,' said Billy.

'For God's sake, Billy!' I said.

'Seven pounds?' Spittles began to slobber. 'Ah, now, boys, boys, boys —'

'Seven pounds,' Billy repeated.

'Are you out of your mind?' I said.

Billy ignored the two of us and watched the bird dab at an old shoe.

'McHugh will give me ten pounds if I ask him,' said Spittles. 'All I have to do is give the word.'

'Seven pounds. Take it or leave it,' said Billy quietly.

'Wait a minute, Billy —' I began.

'Settled!' said Spittles. 'The bird's yours. Give me the money now.'

Billy paid him in single notes. Then he put the cock under his jacket and we left.

'What the hell do you mean by buying a chicken like that!' I said when we were out of earshot. 'You might at least have asked me for my advice. Seven pounds down the drain — that's what that is!'

He stopped at the door of the van and raised his long chin at me.

'You don't have to go halves in this if you don't want to, Tom.'

'It's not the money. Three pounds ten shillings is neither here nor there,' I lied in boast, as I often did with Billy. 'It's just that you might have asked my advice before you took the damned thing.'

'Make up your mind, Tom. You want to go halves or you don't.'

'It's just that I think we could have got a better –'

'Which is it?'

'Here's your money,' I said, thrusting my share into his hand. 'I only hope you know what you're doing.'

'I do,' he said, blinking his lashes at me.

When I told Min of the deal she scolded and sulked and scolded again; and I found myself adopting Billy's tactics with me -- I behaved as if I did not hear her. That set her crazy altogether.

'You'll be away every weekend now!' she accused. 'Have you no thought at all for your family? What sort of a husband and father are you?'

I did not answer.

'Don't you know the neighbours are all laughing at you behind your back?' she went on. 'Hanging on to Billy and Annie as if you had no home of your own! Haven't I borne your children for you? Isn't the house clean? Don't I cook your food and mend your clothes and wear myself out looking after you? Is that not enough for you?'

But I had not Billy's control and I shouted back at her, and for days on end we were at one another's throat. To keep out of her way I spent more and more time at Billy's house after I finished work on the estate.

It was Annie who christened the bird Ginger Hero and it was she who cooked its cornmeal and chopped its hard-boiled eggs and minced its raw meat and rubbed it down each day with ammonia and alcohol. Billy looked after its training and trimmed its hackle and rump feathers. I had no part in its rearing. Indeed, if I as much as mentioned the bird in the house Min lit on me. 'Oh, surely, surely! Mister Thomas, the sporting gentleman with eight children! He's only a labourer on the estate, but he owns a fighting cock, if you don't mind! And what matter if his children can afford butcher's meat only on a Sunday as long as his wee birdie can have the best of fillet steak seven days a week – Fridays and all! What respect can a man like that have for the laws of God when he puts a brute bird before his own family!'

But when the cock began to make a bit of money for us, at Ballybofey and Letterkenny and Strabane, she quit nagging at me and would even bring herself to ask, 'I suppose you'll be travelling somewhere next weekend, will you?' She was not greedy, Min, but she had a powerful regard for money – I suppose because we never had any.

There was no denying that Billy knew how to handle a bird. Six months after we bought that cock from Spittles its own mother would not have recognized it. It was never big and it never weighed a gram over three pounds seven ounces, but it developed great shoulders and a deep chest and a neck of iron, and when you set it in the pit you could see the trembles of the muscles in its legs and feet. But it was none of those things, nor its leather skin, nor its stamina, nor its courage, nor its tenacity, that made it the champion cock of Ireland, but its eyes, its pale calm eyes which revealed nothing, neither anger, nor fear, nor anxiety, nor pain, and which could judge to a fraction of a second when to attack and when to retreat, when to strike and when to withhold, when to swing down those deadly spurs on a stationary head, when to go for the kill.

'The eyes are the best part of him, Billy,' I would say. 'Man, with eyes like that he could tackle a hawk!'

'Maybe, Tom. Maybe,' Billy would say in his calm way.

'I'm not taking away from the work you did on him, mind you. But you'll admit he started off to a great advantage with eyes like that. Didn't he, now?'

And Billy would smile with pleasure, and the ginger tufts on his cheekbones would rise and touch the ends of his sandy lashes.

But although Billy spent one hour every day working with it, and although I had the job of cutting its comb before a main, it was to Annie it would run when the three of us would go out to the pen at the back of the house, and she would sweep it up into her arms, and it would rub its head against her face, and she would coo and whisper into its ear, and it would let itself be pressed against her big breasts, and she would fondle and caress it as if neither Billy nor I were present. I never could tell whether she loved that cock for its own sake, or whether she loved it because it was Billy's; but love it she did, that was clear; and there was no doubt that it was fond of her. But the strange thing about that bird was that it shrank from her every so often, on those days when we had a fight for it. We would go out to the pen as usual and Annie would hold out her arms to it and call to it, 'Ginger! Ginger Hero! Come, boy! Come, come, come!' But it knew, by some strange instinct, that this was a day for the pit, and it would shy away from her and go cautiously to Billy, its head erect, its legs lifting stiffly. She would laugh then, laugh until her whole fat body shook. And she would wag her finger at it and shout raucously, 'You're a bold wee rascal! That's what you are! A naughty wee rogue!' But for all her laughing you could see that she was hurt. And I would wonder, looking at that wary-eyed bird, at the two birds he was and not one at all: Annie's during the week to spoil and pet; and on the morning of a main Billy's bird only, because Billy was the only one of us it would allow to put on its spurs, and Billy alone could set it in the pit – it would have pecked the hands off Annie or me.

It fought eight fights in a row and never lost a feather. It blinded Hoppy Reilly's wee blackie outside Castlederg and killed McHugh's brown cock in five minutes flat at the main at McHugh's own home ground of Frosses. They brought cocks up from Clonmel and they brought cocks down from Inishowen and it scattered them all. Of course, Billy was very careful of it. They tried to get him to pitch the Ginger Hero against two-year-olds and against birds of four pounds and over. Then they tried to persuade him to take part in a Welsh main – a day's contest with eight cocks, the four victors then being paired, then the two – but Billy was having none of that: he knew that they knew that nothing ruins a fighting cock quicker than hacking him like that. (If the bird had been mine I would have agreed because the odds would have been good; and as Ginger won fight after fight and, as his reputation spread, the best we could get was even money.) When everything else failed some of them even reported us to the police. But Spittles Sheridan tipped us off, and the night the police called at Billy's house there was not the trace of a cock to be seen: Annie had it under the blankets with her!

The good times lasted a year. We travelled down to Galway and Mayo, and over to Cavan and Meath, and once – for the sake of a side-bet of thirty pounds – down to Kilkenny to meet a famous white cock that was said to have been reared on raw mackerel and gin. Maybe it was, too. But the day we fought him he must have been in the DTs.

Annie enjoyed the outings as much as any of us. She sat between Billy and me, and laughed, and joked, and waved out to strangers on the roadside, and put her arm round Billy, and rested her head on his shoulder, and sang ballads in her easy voice, and chatted as heedlessly as a schoolgirl. Many a time I found myself watching them in the driver's mirror: Annie's face so relaxed with happiness, Billy's quiet, calm, secretive. And then I would think of Min and myself, and remember our courting days, and wonder with fresh surprise at the way our lives had wilted so rapidly into an endless, ungenerous squabble. And I would be seized by a quick desire to grab Billy and shake him and shout into his ear, 'What sort of a stupid bastard are you? What more do you want? Look at her, man! Look at her!' But I never grabbed him or shook him or shouted at him; and my thoughts invariably shifted from him to her; and many a time I found myself wondering had Min really been the softer of the two in their single days, or had I only imagined that she had been.

That was on the way *to* a fight, when our senses were keen, when we were all three of us alert with anticipation, when the bird could not be touched by anyone but Billy. But on the way home we were always fatigued, and talked little, and the cock was all Annie's again, and she held it in her arms, and stroked it until it fell asleep. Sometimes Annie herself slept, and Billy and I would be left staring at the white columns of the headlights.

'You wouldn't think of selling it?' I asked him the night we drove up from Kilkenny.

Winter was beginning, and the van was cold, and he had taken off his jacket and put it round Annie while she slept.

'Billy!'

'What's that?'

'You wouldn't think of selling, would you?'

I had a vision of me handing over my share to Min and of her stuck for once for something to say.

He shook his head from side to side.

'He's at his prime, I'll grant you,' I said. 'But from now on he won't be getting better.'

'I'm not selling yet,' he said.

'What are you waiting for? Until he's stiff? Until he's lamed or blinded?'

'No, Tom.'

'What, then?'

He took his eyes off the road and looked at me over Annie's sleeping figure.

'I'm going to match him against Captain Robson's Tawny Tiger.'

'You're what!'

'It's all arranged. Next Saturday fortnight, at Grasslough, in County Monaghan.'

'Billy, are you mad? That's not a cock – that's an ostrich! He's a ton weight! There's not a bird in the country would face up to him!'

'It's the only challenge there's left, Tom. Anyhow, there's no point in discussing it. The match is settled.'

'When was it settled? Who settled it? Was I consulted, was I?'

He ignored me.

'I'm going to prove that my bird is as good as the best in the country.'

'*Your* bird!'

He did not even look in my direction.

'I'm going to show them,' he said, almost in a whisper. 'Just you wait and see. I'm going to show them.'

Despite my doubts, or because Billy was never wrong, I decided to put all the savings I had on the Grasslough fight. I asked Min to give me back the rent and housekeeping money for that week. But she refused.

'Gamble the shirt off your back for all I care!' she jeered. 'But the children at least are going to have a roof over their heads and a bite in their mouths.'

Every time we fought now she flung the children at me.

'Look, Min,' I said, 'you'll get your money back. I only want to be able to put on a decent bet.'

'A *decent* bet! That's a good one!'

'All right! Keep it!' I roared.

'I will, Mister Thomas,' she spat back. 'Don't you worry, I will!'

I believe I was angry enough to strike her then. But the children were playing outside the kitchen window. I pulled my coat down from the wall and went across the fields to Billy's house.

Billy was putting the cock into the back of the van and Annie was holding the door open for him. I called and waved to them, and she turned and smiled and waved back to me. She must have had herself harnessed up in all sorts of unaccustomed corsets because I remember noticing how slender and youthful she looked; with her soft, smooth face and her laughing eyes she looked as beautiful as Min had looked the morning I married her. Before I reached them she went into the house.

'All set?' I said to Billy.

'Look, Tom,' he said, glancing quickly after her. 'Will you do me a favour?'

'Surely, Billy.'

'About this fight – and Annie. She thinks it's just an ordinary main. She doesn't know the Tawny Tiger's record. Don't tell her, will you?'

'She must know! She has heard all the talk about him, hasn't she?'

'I'm telling you. She doesn't realize how good he is. If she did she wouldn't want the Hero to be matched against him.'

'But when she sees –'

'You won't tell her, will you?'

Annie came out of the house.

'How long will it take us to get there?' she asked.

'A couple of hours,' said Billy. 'In we get and off we go.'

'I was just looking at you when I was coming up the hill, Annie,' I said. 'It's younger you're getting.'

She gave a peal of laughter.

'Listen to him!' she said, throwing her arms around Billy. 'Why don't you say nice things like that to me?'

He waited until she released him.

'We'll be there before noon,' he said. 'Off we go.'

We climbed into the van and drove off, and Annie never stopped singing until we arrived at Grasslough two hours later.

As soon as I saw Captain Robson my first thought was: Min, if only you were here! Because he was an even finer looking man than Lord Downside, and she thought Downside was the finest gentleman in the world. He was English, well over six feet, straight as a rush, and dressed in an elegant dark suit and a canary waistcoat. He invited us into his house for drinks and discussed the fight – he called it 'the duel' – as briskly as if he were planning a day's harvesting; no winking, no nudging, no mumbling behind the backs of hands, no nervousness of a police raid, no sly questions about age or weight or diet. We had never seen anything like this before. Annie looked about her with big wondrous eyes. Even the cool Billy was impressed. I let him do all the talking.

Then the Captain brought us out to a huge hay shed and showed us his pit.

'It is regulation,' he said. 'Usual eighteen feet in diameter. Surround sixteen inches high. Sawdust floor. Satisfactory?'

'Grand,' said Billy.

'Good. Now we'll have a look at Tawny Tiger.'

He cracked his fingers and a workman, who had been standing at a distance, came running up.

'Fetch the Tiger, O'Boyle,' he said, and O'Boyle scuttled off.

'I've been thinking about this duel,' he went on. 'And I've come to the conclusion that it isn't fair to ask you to risk your bird against a heavier and more experienced cock.'

'We're agreeable to –' Billy began.

'No, it is not fair. So in the circumstances, since this is more a contest for prestige, I have made two decisions: there will be no gambling on this duel; but if your bird wins I will give you two hundred pounds; and if I win I will be amply rewarded by knowing that I own the best cock in Ireland. Satisfactory?'

'Suits me,' said Billy.

'And your friend?' said the Captain.

'Suits me,' I said, because that was what Billy had said.

'Good. O'Boyle will be judge. I can vouch for his integrity. Let's get started, shall we?'

Annie stood between Billy and me at the edge of the pit. She had not opened her mouth since we had arrived at Robson's place. Now she murmured something to Billy but he did not answer her. He had our cock under his jacket and he was stroking it slowly and deliberately as if he were conveying last minute instructions to it. She turned to me.

'Tom –' she spoke in a whisper.

'What is it?'

'I – I – have a queer feeling about this place.'

'It will be all over in no time,' I said.

'It's the Hero I'm thinking about. Will he be hurt, Tom?'

I pretended to laugh. 'Hurt? He won't even be tickled!'

'Could we call it off, Tom? Is it too late to call it off?'

'Easy, Annie. Easy. There's nothing to worry about.'

She did not hear what I said. Her lips were parted and her breath was coming in shallow gasps, and her eyes roamed anxiously around that great shed as if she were taking a mental note of the exits.

My heart sank when I saw the size of Tawny Tiger, and when Ginger Hero was set in the pit the Captain's bird seemed to grow even bigger. It was no consolation that at last Billy had made a mistake. I would willingly have surrendered the money that was sweating in my pocket if I could have grabbed our bird and run out of that eerie shed that echoed and re-echoed in its high roof with every tiny sound that was made under it. Not that there was much noise; only a few clipped words from the Captain, and the starting order from O'Boyle – 'Let the cocks fight.' Until that moment I never knew how much I loved the familiar hissing and booing and cheering and squabbling and the vulgar comments and the swearing. This orderly, superior set-up was no sport. It was unnatural.

The Tiger barged into battle, wings wide, neck arched, eyes burning, body high and poised. Ginger Hero crouched, waiting, his eyes dead, watchful, wary. For a second they were three feet apart; then, simultaneously, they attacked. There was the dull thud of their bodies, the click of spur against spur, and the Hero was bowled over. At first I could see nothing but the broad back of the Tiger, and its plunging head, and its stabbing feet. I thought: My God, it has punctured the Hero's throat! But then I saw our cock's legs working like pistons, scratching, scratching at the Tiger's breast; the spurs were not sticking, could not penetrate the feathers and skin; but although the Tiger was mauling his head and neck, those never stopped working until the left spur penetrated, and the Tiger was flung from his dominance.

I looked at Annie. Her hands were pressed to the sides of her head. I glanced beyond her to Billy. He might have been asleep, so calm he looked. Then I saw his lips moving, and heard him breathe. 'Yes. Yes. Yes. Yes. Yes. Yes —' without ceasing, almost inaudibly, as if he were praying devoutly.

The first blood was drawn. It flowed from below the Hero's right eye. But before I could take a closer look they were battling again.

The Tiger made his second charge, but this time our bird kept his feet. Then they both went down, spurs locked, necks linked, two balls of feathers rolling over and over. The Hero freed himself first, caught the Tiger's head still for an unguarded second, and spiked it with such force that, for the moment those tiny needles gored into the Tiger, our bird was levered two feet into the air.

It was then that the Tawny Tiger went mad, so mad that he turned his back on our cock, and went tearing around the circumference of the pit, with his great blazing head straining to the roof, and his wings trailing through the sawdust, and his beak open and emitting a throaty, hissing sound. He was so mad that he did not know where he was or what it was he was supposed to be doing. Then, suddenly, he remembered. He stopped at the head of the pit, surveyed the ring, spotted the Hero and, with a cry that was almost human in its abandon, half-flew, half-raced at our cock. They met in the centre of the pit, and there – without once separating again – they spiked and speared and stabbed and savaged one another with all the concentrated fury that was in them.

I did not watch all of it. For the first time in my life I felt sickened by it. There, in the silence of that shed, with no sound but the odd quick squawk of sudden pain and the sibilant 'Yes. Yes. Yes. Yes –' of Billy, with no cheering, no laughing, no fun, no ribaldry, that savage deadly battle for life was too tense, too heartless. Sometimes I closed my eyes. Sometimes I looked at Annie. Her hands never left her head; her body was as motionless as a statue. Sometimes I watched the Captain's pale, evil face – for now it was evil. Sometimes I looked at O'Boyle. But always my gaze went back to the cocks. They were spent now. Only their endless courage kept them going, kept them plunging at each other.

The Tawny Tiger was on his side. The brownish-yellow feathers of his body were wet and splashed with sawdust, and his neck, almost naked, glistened like raw meat. His legs were stiff and quivering.

Over him stood our tattered cock. He balanced on his left foot, and with his right he spiked the head of his opponent with slow, drunken, involuntary movements. He was scarcely able to stand but he kept on spiking as if that were the only movement he was capable of.

Annie's scream shattered the muted silence of that shed. Her hands went up to her hair; she flung her head back; her mouth opened; and a wild, animal cry broke from her lips. It was a wail of terrible agony.

'Stop it!' she moaned. 'Stop it! Stop it! Stop it!'

I gripped her arm.

'Annie! Annie!'

She shook me off and fell on Billy, pounding his shoulders with her fists.

'Stop it!' she screamed. 'Stop it! Stop it! Stop it! Stop it!'

He did not feel the first blows, so engrossed was he in the fight. Then his eyes darted to her for a second –

'Take her away, for Christ's sake!' he muttered to me – and went back to the ring again.

I tried to hold her arms but she had the strength of three women. She clawed at his neck and shoulders and tried to push him into the pit.

'Take her away! She'll ruin everything!' he snapped. 'Take her away!'

'Stop it, Billy! Oh, God, stop it, Billy! Please, Billy. Please!'

He swung on her then, his face stretched with fury, put his two hands against her body, and flung her violently back from him. She fell on the floor behind him. He wheeled back to watch the end of the fight. She lay there, sobbing.

I lifted her gently off the ground and led her, trembling, out of the shed. We passed the Captain and O'Boyle. They did not see us although we came between them and the pit.

Since we had married I had never seen Min cry. When she should have cried she had jeered or sulked. And now, with Annie, I was awkward and fumbling. I took her to the back of the van, and climbed in beside her, and spoke to her as I had not spoken since my courting days. Her teeth were chattering and she clung to me. I held her to me, and whispered to her, and covered her face with gentle kisses, and stroked her smooth, soft face with my rough hands. The sobbing stopped. And then, fiercely, wildly, she pulled me to her, and kissed me again and again. And in the moment before the singing blood drowned my thinking I imagined I heard her say, 'Billy, Billy, Billy —'

We were sitting in the front when Billy joined us. The cock lay on its side on the upturned palms of his hands. Its feet were still stabbing the empty air.

'It's all over! He won! He won!' Billy was breathless with triumph. 'Quick! Where's the brandy?'

'It's in the back, Billy,' I said.

He held the cock out to Annie.

'There, Annie. He's yours now.'

'No,' she said coldly, turning her face away. 'No, no, no. Not today.'

He looked quickly at her and then at me. His cheekbones went up and his eyes went wary. You never could tell what Billy was thinking.

'Give the cock to me,' I said quickly, because his steady eyes were probing me and I was embarrassed.

I took the bird from him and pretended to examine its wounds. Billy still stood looking in at us.

'I'll be back shortly,' he said at length. 'The Captain is counting out the prize money.'

I climbed into the back and washed the bird in alcohol. Its eyes were glazed and its heartbeat irregular. I knew it would be dead before we got home but I did all the jobs to it as tenderly as Annie would have done them.

'Will you tell Billy?' I said to her.

She sat staring straight in front of her.

'It doesn't matter,' she said.

'I believe he suspects,' I said.

'It doesn't matter, Tom,' she said. 'It doesn't matter at all.'

Then Billy came back and tossed a roll of notes on to my knees.

'How is he?' he asked.

'Fair. Only fair.'

He looked at Annie.

'I'm – I'm sorry I lost my temper back there.'

She snorted through her nose.

'Let's get home,' she said irritably. 'It's a long journey.'

His eyelashes fluttered. He smiled uncertainly.

'Home it is,' he said. 'Home it is.' And he started up the engine.

On our way through the town of Omagh I heard the sound of the cock's feet scraping the side of the van and I knew it was his dying kick. But I said nothing to the others because none of us had spoken since the journey had begun, and because I knew they must have heard the sound too.

Three weeks later Billy got a job as land steward on an estate in the south of England and Annie and himself left Donegal for good. Min sent them a card that first Christmas, but they did not reply. We never heard from them again. The parish priest told me, one Sunday after Mass, that he had had a letter from Annie asking for a copy of her marriage certificate.

'Must be a christening in the family,' he said. 'Takes the English air!' And he smiled roguishly. I did not tell Min.

With my share of the winnings of the Grasslough fight she had opened a small shop in the shed beside the house. She sold ice cream and groceries and sweets to the families who lived on the estate. There was little profit in it – on a good week she made two pounds clear and she would boast, 'Between us we're making as much as the land steward now!' – but getting away from the kitchen and the children, and meeting the neighbours, and chatting to them made a new woman of her. She put on weight, and her face lost some of its creases. And every night, when I got home from work, she sat opposite me on the other side of the fire and told me all the gossip of the countryside. She was always a good mimic, Min, and many a night she had me in stitches laughing at her.

She tried to persuade me to take up cockfighting again; 'A man needs a hobby,' she said. But I had had enough of cocks.

'I tell you what, then, Tom,' she said, her face lighting up. 'We'll call this shop after that bird of yours – what's this his name was? – Ginger Love? – Ginger Hope?'

'Ginger Hero,' I said.

'That's it!' she laughed girlishly. 'We'll call the shop The Ginger Hero – so that we'll never forget that it was him that turned our luck!'

'Right, Min,' I said. 'The Ginger Hero it will be.'

And the next day – it was a Saturday – I bought a tin of black paint and a length of timber, and printed the three words as steadily and as evenly as I was able.

A Man's World

I had five maiden aunts and they doted on me. I was their only
nephew, the child of their youngest sister, Christina, who alone
of the whole family of twelve left home while she was still in her
teens to work in the nearest town of Strabane and married a town
man. The others stayed together, grew into men and women,
buried Grandfather and Grandmother (whom I never knew) and
the six brothers (whom I never knew either) who must have died
long before their time. When I first became aware of them they
were settled women whose ages ranged from about forty-five to
fifty, each with her role in the running of their doll's house. Aunt
Kate and Aunt Maggie were the breadwinners, teachers in the
village school; Aunt Agnes was the housekeeper; Aunt Sarah
looked after the cow and the chickens and the precise garden; and
Aunt Rose – well, as the others used to say with gentle tolerance,
'Rose will always be Rose'. That was good enough for me.

Every year on August 1st we went to Donegal to visit them.
The journey itself was an adventure in a mad scarlet rail-bus
which plunged along a narrow-gauge track pulling a dancing
wagon of luggage behind it and emitted a throaty *toot-toot* now
and again just for the sheer joy of it. It was a two-and-a-half hour
trip through hills and between mountains, past lakes and streams,
between high banks glowing with sun-yellow whins and flat
boglands of purple and brown and russet. Inside the bus country
women, anonymous in black head shawls, and great, unshaven
country men chatted volubly to one another, and the atmosphere
took body with the pungent smoke of their pipes. Then at the end
of the line, run to earth at the foot of grey mountains, the village
of Ardara itself, a hamlet of about four hundred people. The line

stopped abruptly half a mile short of the village, although why, after battling across impossible terrain for the previous sixty miles, it could not tackle the last soggy stretch used to puzzle me. But that was its unpredictable way and we had no reason to complain because Mother's home was only a stone's throw away from the terminus.

For days before we would leave home Father would be quiet and moody and I never remember a holiday that was not overshadowed by his cold withdrawal from our enthusiastic preparations. But once we were on our way he thawed slowly, partly because of the whiskey flask he carried in his hip pocket and partly because of Mother's watchful attentions to him. So that by the time the rail-bus stuttered to a halt he had arrived at a state of garrulous good humour. And there on the platform would be the five aunts, smiling, happy, nervous, welcoming, one or two of them very often in slippers and aprons if the rail-bus caught them unawares, bobbing up and down in the golden heat of an August afternoon.

Of course I got their first attention. Invariably I had got bigger and fatter and healthier and more manly and cleverer – that on a second's observation – and before we had left the station, but not before I had been handled by each aunt in turn, it was unanimous that I was 'more a caution than ever'. Mother came next. Less said now but five pairs of eyes quickly noted the shoulders gathering flesh and the new line at the edge of the mouth and there were tentative, casual-sounding questions about how she was eating and sleeping. Lastly, Father. They did love him, I believe now, because he was Christina's husband and the father of her child. But he was a man – more, a town man – and since they had no experience of men they had nothing spontaneous to say to him and had to improvise with formalities. To tide the situation over Father usually busied himself by passing me from one to the other.

The first few days of the holiday were never enjoyable: I had to go over every song and recitation and mime and imitation that I had done in previous summers (every detail had to be perfect, too) and then bring them up to date with the latest additions to my repertoire, not once but half a dozen times until Aunt Sarah or Aunt Agnes would insist that the others were tiring me and Aunt Kate and Aunt Maggie would finally agree to release me. If I were singing Mother would accompany me on the yellow-keyed piano, half of whose notes were mute, and her eyes would rove restlessly round the five naked faces, smiling brightly if a sister's eyes met hers or just moving from one to the other as if she were somehow playing them and not the piano. At last I would be set free, out to the fields and the Atlantic wind and to Aunt Rose.

It was always a relief to get away from them and yet when I would run round to the back of the house and stand looking across the valley towards the hazel wood where the witch with the red eyes lived I was neither surprised nor disappointed to find Aunt Rose there before me, waiting for me. I know now, after almost thirty years, that she was a plain-looking woman. Her face was too white, her cheeks too flat, her mouth permanently open, her head shot forward. But at five or six years of age I saw only a mild woman who always smiled and seldom spoke and knew exactly what would delight a boy of my age. There would be a black rabbit in the warren or a pigeon's nest in the wood or a hedgehog along the path beside the burn or a rose tree, sudden and inexplicable, in the lower meadow. Or she had spotted an early crop of nuts and had guarded it for me by her silence. Or she had a sick hen in the byre with a ludicrous bandage of cotton wool tied round its head or a trunkful of mysteries sent home from Kenya by some granduncle who had a wandering foot. And all these things she would reveal to me, not exultantly but almost coyly, like a fresh girl wooing her first youth. Unless we were far out of earshot of the house, away beyond the hazel wood, for example, where the boglands stretched out before us and we had to raise our voices to be heard above the wind or in the sweet-smelling secrecy of the byre where a whisper would do: in those places she talked, wildly, carelessly, senselessly it seemed to me a lot of the time, telling me about Grandfather and Grandmother and about her schooldays and about a necklace she once bought with egg money and about a fortune teller who promised great things for her. Sometimes, too, she would talk about her dead brothers. I was too young to invest their unexplained passing with mystery and too incurious to ask questions about them. I knew only the details Aunt Kate or Aunt Maggie had volunteered – that the family had stopped keeping bees when Uncle John died or that the good bedroom could not be used for displaying Mother's wedding gifts because Uncle Joe was lying there in his last illness – so that I had accepted these men as shadowy backgrounds to memorable events in the family. But Aunt Rose talked about them, giving them girth and height and colouring, made me laugh at Uncle Peter's attempt to train a sheep dog or Uncle Pat's efforts at changing the course of the burn. And once, I remember, after she had led me through Uncle Jim's career as a fighting patriot and I, hoping for a dramatic conclusion to the tale, had asked her how did he die, the question genuinely puzzled her. She thought for a moment and said, 'I don't know – I just suppose he died.' The problem interested her as much as it interested me, no more, no less.

When she and I would get back to the house again we would find Mother and the other four basking in the sun at the gable. Aunt Kate would say, 'And where has Rose been hiding our young man? Eh? Keeping him to herself, I'll bet. Aye, Rose is a deep one.' And there would be a sympathetic laugh.

Father spent most of his day in the village. After a late breakfast he would say, 'I think I'll go out and stretch my legs and leave you women to your gossiping.' We would not see him again until lunchtime when he would sit at the head of the table and make laborious jokes about men in the village who, he said, had asked him to 'put in a good word with the girls'. Mother would tell him sharply to shut up. But he would persist. With the best of good humour he would point out the many advantages of a match between Aunt Maggie, for example, and Jimmy the Post who owned one of the best-cared-for farms in the locality. 'It's a proposition,' he would say, slapping the table with his fingertips. 'Turn it over. Give it a thought.' Occasionally when he continued his schemes after lunch Mother would accuse him of being drunk. He would then go sullenly to bed for the remainder of the afternoon and a silence would fall on the house. Only Aunt Rose seemed to be unaware of the undercurrents which even I was beginning to understand.

On the eve of my eighth birthday Father was sacked from his job in the civil service. His Christmas binge had extended too far into January and his superiors had no patience left. However, as a return for twenty years' service, they promised him the first offer of any substitute work which might arise during the year through illness. When our meagre savings were exhausted three weeks after Father's dismissal there was nothing for us but appeal to the aunts. Mother wrote to them and by return post came an enthusiastic invitation to us to come and stay as long as we wished. The following afternoon we set off.

Never before had I travelled to Ardara in the winter and the journey was a series of disappointments. Darkness caught up with us before we were half way and snow began to fall. The red rail-bus was cold and feebly lit and the other passengers hugged themselves in silence in scattered seats. A cattle dealer behind me smoked a dirty clay pipe whose fumes sickened me. Mother sat upright beside me, her hands up her sleeves, hissing a rosary to herself, and Father slept heavily somewhere at the rear. Only the happiness that I knew lay ahead kept me from whining.

The five aunts were on the platform to meet us and everything was suddenly right again. They were friendlier than ever and even more talkative. Although it was only five months since they had last seen me they agreed that I had got bigger and firmer and, when they hugged me in turn, each of them held on to me protectively for a second longer than usual. Indeed they scarcely looked at Mother at all, so concentrated were they on me. But to Father they were as welcoming and as polite as ever. They told him he was looking very well and said that January was a good time for a rest. All bundled together, all talking at the same time, the eight of us walked the short distance to the house.

That night and for the next three days snow kept falling. Gradually paths, roadways, hedges became one. The village school was closed and Aunt Kate and Aunt Maggie were at home all day. Only Father ventured out, beating an unsteady path for himself to the town. In the house talk became thin. There would be hours of quiet and then from upstairs would come the sharp voices raised in anger of two of the aunts. Sometimes they snapped at one another when we were all together and on those occasions Mother would tell me to go to the sitting room and 'keep up with your lessons'. I noticed that she had begun doing most of the heavy housework; never before had she been allowed to lift a finger.

Ardara was turning sour for me. I could not go outside because of the snow drifts and inside I was either forgotten about or the object of everybody's attention. Perhaps for a whole morning I would moon about, unseen, and then suddenly a couple of the women would decide that my education was being neglected. Aunt Kate and Mother would lead me to the sitting room, set me between them and begin teaching me. These lessons frequently ended in tears. Aunt Kate would call me stubborn and obstinate and spoiled and Mother would defend me; or Aunt Kate would stump off in disgust and Mother would suddenly slap my cheeks with her open hand, something she used never to do. To get away from them all I would creep into Father's bed and lie beside him, warm and snoring. When he would awaken and dress himself fumblingly for the village I would move into the part of the bed warmed by his body and wait until he came back again. Sometimes in his sleep he would throw his hand across my chest and I would lie motionless beneath it, admiring its roughness.

By the end of two weeks I knew I hated my five aunts, Rose especially because she had disappointed me the most. I had expected her to provide some entertainment, to have something of interest tucked away. But she had nothing; the snow had covered all her resources. Yet she kept haunting me. Wherever I went in the small house she followed me, watching me with her diluted blue eyes, her head shot forward, her mouth never closed, silent. When I would look back arrogantly at her the flat cheeks would rise in a smile and her head would bob up and down in greeting but she had nothing to say. Even when I thought she was out in the byre or bringing in turf for the fire I would discover her pale face pressed against the window, peering in at me. I began to ignore her; but that made no difference. At last, in desperation one day, I called her 'cow face', the most hurtful nickname I would concoct, and that rid me of her. From then on she stopped following me, but whenever we were together in the kitchen or the sitting room I could feel her eyes on me.

It was one of the railway men who found Father lying unconscious in a drift of snow at the side of the signal box. He carried him on his shoulders to the house and then went for the doctor. I was in Father's bed waiting for him to come back when the dark bulk of the two men passed the window. The house became suddenly quick with talk again. Mother was purposeful and competent and organized the aunts who were racing around in near-hysteria. They laid him in his bed and loaded him with blankets. His lips were blue, I remember, and one eye open and one shut in a grotesque wink. If he dies, I thought, I want to die too; I don't want to be the only man left in this house. But Mother did not let him die. Until the doctor came, hours later, she sat beside him, pouring drops of brandy into his mouth, rubbing his feet and legs and cheeks with her strong hands, talking to him with quiet intensity, calling him back to life. When the doctor arrived and I was chased out of the way I went out to the byre to lie down and die too.

Aunt Rose interrupted me. I should have locked the door from the inside. 'Is it you?' she said, peering into the dark corner where I lay on damp straw.

'Why?'

'I just thought it was you.' She came over to me and squatted down beside me. 'What are you doing here?'

'Nothing.'

'It's the snow,' she said, half to herself. 'The snow.'

The cold was seeping through my clothes. My lips must be darkening by now.

'I'll take you over to the brook and show you McHugh's new lambs.'

'No.'

'We'll go to the village – no one will miss us now – and buy a poke of sweets.'

'Go away.'

'You never saw Uncle John's sun helmet. It's up in the loft. Come on up and we'll look at it.'

'Go away. Go away.' I closed one eye and waited for death to take me.

'I'll show you something,' she said softly, 'if you promise not to tell no one.'

'I don't want to see anything.'

'No one knows about this. No one in the whole world except me.'

I sat up, interested. I could die later. 'Tell me what it is first.'

'Promise?'

'Promise.'

She rose to her feet. Her face, now robbed of its perpetual smile, seemed strange, almost intelligent. She went over to the door and bolted it. Then her fingers groped along the lintel above the window, found a loose stone and removed it. From the hole she brought out a scrap of paper. I got up and stood behind her.

'There,' she said. 'Read that.' It was a letter. Her hands were trembling.

The byre was dark and the handwriting spidery but I made it out. The letter was headed by an address in Boston and dated 1906. 'Dear Rose,' it said, 'I have now made enough money for your passage. If you will come out and marry me I will send it to you. Please make up your mind and reply by return. In haste, Bill Sweeney.'

'Is that the whole surprise?' I asked, disappointed.

She took the letter from me, folded it and put it back in its hiding place. 'Bald Billy they called him,' she said. 'Because even then he hadn't a stab of hair on his head.' She drew back the bolt on the door and stood looking across the stunted hedge into the snow-covered meadow. The smile was creeping back into her face as she went out into the crisp air.

Father was out of his bed of pneumonia within a fortnight and well enough to accept a temporary post in early March. The fright did him good. We left Ardara when spring was imminent and as I sat waiting impatiently for the rail-bus to pull out of the station the five faces of the aunts smiled and nodded in at us as if nothing had happened. But I knew then that this was a man's world and I was determined to go camping with the boys next August. There was nothing to bring me back there anymore, nothing to interest me, not even Aunt Rose.

Among the Ruins

There was no doubt about it, Joe thought, as he sat in the car and waited for his wife and children to join him: Margo was simply wonderful. She had had an early lunch for them; she had so cleverly primed the children – who usually detested these organized outings with their parents – that they were still curious about the destination, and eager to be off. The whole idea of going back to Corradinna had been hers and, although it was early summer and the weather would probably have been good anyhow, she had managed to choose the best Sunday of the year so far. Yes, Margo was simply wonderful.

When she had first mentioned her plan to him the previous Friday night he felt unaccountably stubborn. 'Corradinna? What the hell would take us there? There's nothing there now but the ruins of the old place.'

'You still must have some curiosity about it,' she had urged. 'Even if it's only to see if you have lost the feel of the place.'

'Feel?' he had said, deliberately misunderstanding her. 'You know me – I'm not sentimental that way.'

'And for the children's sake, too. I would like them to see where you lived when you were their age. It would be good for them.'

'I don't see the point,' he had said. 'I don't see the point at all.'

But she had persisted, and that night and the next day his stubbornness gave way to a stirring of memory and then to a surprising excitement that revealed itself in his silence and his foolish grin. And now that they were about to set off there was added a great surge of gratitude to her for tapping this forgotten source of joy in him. She knew and understood him so well.

Mary and Peter sat impatiently on the edge of the back seat. She was her mother in miniature.

'Now, Mammy! Where? Where?' she begged. 'You promised you would tell us now.'

Margo turned to watch their faces. 'We are going to Donegal –'

'I want to go to the beach,' Peter broke in.

'– to see where your Daddy used to live and play when he was your age.'

'Are we, Daddy? Really?' Mary asked.

'Looks like it,' said Joe, smiling helplessly.

'I still want to go to the beach,' said Peter doggedly.

Mary caught his arm. 'Can't you hear, stupid? We're going to see where Daddy used to play when he was a little boy.'

'Where's that?' Peter asked cautiously.

'Away, away far off in Donegal,' said Margo. 'And if you're going to behave like that you are going to spoil the day on all of us.'

'So stop whining, boy!' said Mary severely, imitating her mother with unconscious accuracy.

'I'm not whining.'

'You were a minute ago.'

'That'll do, the both of you! Do you want to ruin the day on your Daddy?'

'What's the name of the place?' Mary asked.

'Corradinna,' said Joe.

'Corradinna,' said Peter, sampling the word. 'That's a funny name.' He turned to his sister, screwed up his face and said in a man's voice, 'Corradinna.'

'Corradinna,' she piped back at him.

They fell into a fit of laughing at their private joke.

After the first hour they became restless. They changed sides – Mary behind Margo and Peter behind Joe. Later they changed back again. Then they quarrelled over the exact position of the imaginary line down the middle of the back seat. Then Peter wanted the windows down and Mary wanted them up; she was cold, she said. Then Margo asked Joe to pull in to the side because Peter had to go out for a minute. Then, five miles farther on, Mary had to get out. It was the usual pattern for a Sunday afternoon outing, but today it did not irk Joe because Margo had assumed complete control, soothing, compromising, reprimanding, keeping peace, and the children's bickering claimed only a fraction of his attention. She was allowing him the uninterrupted luxury of remembering, hearing sounds and voices and cries he thought he had forgotten.

Corradinna lay at the foot of Errigal mountain, a pyramid of granite that rose three thousand feet out of the black bog earth. Because it marked the end of their journey and was visible for the last twenty miles Joe found himself leaning over the driving wheel, as if to see beyond the folds of hills that still lay before him.

'Easy,' said Margo. 'You're going too fast.'

'Am I?'

'You'll be there time enough. Do you want the children to get sick?'

At this moment I don't give a damn, he thought without callousness; at this moment, with Meenalaragan and Pigeon Top on my left and Glenmakennif and Altanure on my right. Because these are my hills and I knew them before I knew wife or children.

'Joe! Do you hear me?'

'Sorry,' he said, slowing down. 'Sorry.'

Every Saturday morning, with the two Lakeland terriers, just for a walk. You got to the top of one hill and stood there with your arms opened out to the wind and watched the dogs, crazed with the scent of a fox, scramble down before you, and you ran down after them and then up the next incline and down the next and up and down and up and down, and when you got home in time for dinner the dogs were so fatigued that they could not sleep but lay restlessly on the cold flags of the kitchen floor, staining the stone under their noses with circles of damp. It is all coming back to me, he thought.

They left the car at the side of the road and walked up the grass-covered track to the ruins of the house. The roof had fallen in and the windows were holes in the walls. Someone had carved his initials on the doorpost: 'J.M . . . NOV. 1941.' Mary, convinced that there must still be something spectacular to be seen after so long a journey, began asking petulantly, 'Show us now, Mammy! Show us now!'

'This is it all,' Margo said. 'This is where your Daddy used to play.'

'Who did he play with? What games did he play?'

'He used to play around the house here. And around those fields. Why don't you and Peter go exploring for yourselves, while your Daddy and I look around here?'

'I have seen everything,' said Peter.

'You couldn't have,' said Margo. 'Go on, off with the pair of you! Your Daddy and I will be around here somewhere. And if you get tired walking go and sit in the car.'

When they had gone she said to Joe, 'Was that the garden?'

'Yes,' he said, and walked away from her. She followed him.

The garden, the path, the gooseberry tree. And the chestnut. That is our swing. Our father ties the ropes across that branch, and we soar up and out over the laneway. And Mother cries, 'Careful, Joe! Careful!' and Susan, my sister, squeals, 'Higher! Higher!' and Father comes round the side of the house and says, 'Is the cow not in yet, boy?' and Susan says, 'I'll get it, Joe's busy swinging.' Off she runs like a fairy thing, and because she is gone, the boy who is I jumps down and runs after her, and when he catches up with her they dawdle along the bank of the river – river? What river? This trickle of water? Where did the river go? – and he says, 'Dare you to jump the river.' 'How much?' 'Half the hazelnuts under my bed.' 'It's a bet.' And she grips her lips between her teeth and takes a wild, gangling leap and lands in the middle of the water. They laugh and take off her shoes and wring out her socks and, the wetting suddenly forgotten, stroll across the fields to the wood – but where is the wood? It couldn't be this sad little cluster of oaks! – until they come to the bluebell patch. 'We'll bring home bluebells to Mother.' Susan's arms are out. 'Fill them,' she says. 'No. These will do.' 'Fill them. Fill them.' 'We forgot the cow.' 'The cow! Quick. The cow!' Another race across the meadow, through the gap in the hedge, clean over the river this time, because there is no bet to tighten your legs. And home, home, back past the barn. The barn, with its treasures – parts of bicycles, bits of bee-hives, a tea chest of old clothes, the drumsticks. Susan sings and he accompanies her with the drumsticks on a cigar box. She dresses up in a long, tan-coloured silk frock, strap-over shoes, a huge picture hat – all her mother's. She sings, 'Red sails in the sunset,' over and over again, because the first line is the only one she knows.

'Susan! Joe! Teatime!'

Hide! Hide! Down to the bower at the foot of the garden! Oh, the laughing in that bower! Laughing till they are sore. And then, as soon as they sober up, one of them pulls a face, and they are off again. Oh, God, the pain of that laughing! 'What do you two laugh at?' Father says. 'You would think to look at you that you were a pair of halfwits. What *do* you laugh at, anyhow?' And that makes them worse, because Susan twitches her eyes or shrugs her shoulders, and if they were to be killed they couldn't stop now at all.

'Joe?' Margo's voice at his elbow. 'What are you smiling at, Joe?'

Suddenly he was alert, wary. 'Remembering,' he said.

'Remembering what?'

'The bower. Susan and myself in the bower.'

'What was it?'

'A place – a sort of hideout at the foot of the garden there. It's gone now. I looked.'

'What did you do there?'

'Laugh. Laugh, mostly.'

Clouds had come up from the west and hidden the sun and the air was cold.

'What did you laugh at?'

'I don't know. We just laughed. We called it the laughing house.'

'But you must have been laughing *at* something,' she persisted. 'Did you make jokes for one another?'

'No, no, no. No jokes. Not laughing like that. Just – just silly laughing.'

'Still there must have been something to laugh at, even for silly laughing, as you call it. What sort of silly things used you laugh at?'

'What did we laugh at?' An explanation was necessary. We must have laughed at something. There must have been something that triggered it off.

'Are you not going to tell me?' Margo's face had sharpened. She stood before him, insisting on a revelation.

'Susan and I –' he mumbled.

'I know,' she said quickly. 'Susan and you in the bower. Once you got there together you laughed your heads off. And I want to know what you laughed *at*.'

'She would make up a word – any word, any silly-sounding word – and that would set us off,' he said clutching at the first faint memory that occurred to him. 'Some silly word like – like "sligalog", or "skookalook". That sort of thing.'

' "Skookalook". What's funny about that?'

'I don't know if that was one of them. I meant just any made-up word at all. In there, in the bower, somehow it seemed to sound – so funny.'

'And that's all?'

'That was all,' he said limply.

Relenting, now that he had admitted her to these privacies, she put her arm through his and rubbed her cheek against his sleeve. 'Poor Joe,' she said. 'Poor silly, simple Joe. Come on, let's go for a walk. It will soon be time to head home again.'

Later, when they got back to the car, they found Mary sitting alone in the back seat. 'What kept you two?' the child demanded in the stern voice they used to laugh at a few years ago.

'Where's Peter?' Margo asked.

'I don't know. We're not speaking,' said Mary primly. 'He has been gone for over half-an-hour.'

'I'll get him,' Joe volunteered. 'He won't be far away.'

'Will I go with you?'

'No. I'll be quicker alone,' said Joe. He felt that Margo knew he was glad of the opportunity to have a last look around by himself. 'Start the motor and turn on the heater,' he called back. 'There is a dew falling.'

He did not look for the boy. He walked slowly up the path to the remains of the house and walked round them once, twice, three times. He tried to move without making any sound so that the stillness in his mind would not be disturbed. He knew he was waiting for something. But nothing came from the past – no voice, no cry, no laugh, not even the bark of a dog. He was suddenly angry. He charged down the garden and through the hedge. 'Peter!' he shouted. 'Peter! Peter!'

The echoes of his voice mocked him.

'Peter! Peter!'

Now panic gripped him. The child had had an accident! He broke into a run, crossed the lower meadow, leaped the stream and ran up the incline to the cluster of trees. 'Peter? Peter!'

Peter was so engrossed in his play that he was not aware of his father until Joe caught him by the shoulder and shook him. He was on his knees at the mouth of a rabbit hole, sticking small twigs into the soft earth.

'Peter! What the hell!'

'Look, Daddy. Look! I'm donging the tower!'

'Did you not hear me shouting? Are you deaf?'

'Let me stay, Daddy. I'll have the tower donged in another five minutes.'

'Come on!' Joe dragged him away. 'Your mother will think we're both lost. Such a fright I got! Calling all over the place. Hurry up!'

'Please, Daddy, let me stay for –'

'Now, I said! It will be long past your bedtime when we get back.'

Until they got to the road Peter had to trot to keep up with him. 'Here he is!' Joe announced. 'Playing games by himself in the wood!' Margo and Mary were listening to the radio. 'Let's get started,' said Margo. 'I'm sleepy.'

'Calling and calling, and the little blighter wouldn't even answer me!'

'Your feet are wet,' said Margo.

'That won't kill me,' said Joe gruffly.

Margo said something but he pressed the starter and revved up the engine so that her voice was drowned.

On the way home a sense of aloneness crept over him. Once he gave in to the temptation to glance in the mirror but it was already dark outside, and Errigal was just part of the blackness behind them. He should never have gone back with Margo and the children. Because the past is a mirage – a soft illusion into which one steps in order to escape the present. Like hiding in the bower. How could he have told Margo that the bower had been their retreat, Susan's and his, their laughing house? The dank little den that smelled of damp and decay which let in no sunlight and kept out no rain? Was that their retreat? And, if it came to that, how often had they laughed there? Did they not bicker and fight all the time, like Peter and Mary? 'I'll tell on you, boy. I'll tell Mammy on you.' Susan's petulant voice came back to him now, clearer and harsher than the other memories.

'Go and tell, then, old telltale.'

'I'm going now. I'm going now. And you'll get a beating, boy, when you come in for your tea.'

'Telltale!'

'Bully!'

How sharply he remembered: walking alone and desolate along the bottom of the meadow, imagining the stories Susan was telling their father and mother in the house, knowing that eventually he would have to go up and face the accusation and his father's hard eyes and his mother's hard mouth, how he would stammer out his side of the story and then take his beating, and then be sent to bed. Was that his childhood? Why, Joe wondered, had he been so excited about the trip that morning? What had he expected to find at Corradinna – a restoration of innocence? A dream confirmed? He could not remember. All he knew now was that the visit had been a mistake. It had robbed him of a precious thing, his illusions of his past, and in their place now there was nothing – nothing at all but the truth.

'Aow! Aow! Peter nipped me! Peter nipped me!' Mary's cry shattered the sleepy quiet in the car.

'What's the matter with you?' asked Margo.

'Peter, Mammy. He nipped me in the arm! Ah, my arm! My arm!' She made no effort to control her tears.

'She kicked me first,' said Peter. 'She kicked my ankle.'

'I didn't, Mammy! I didn't. Ah-ah-ah-ah! It's bleeding! I can feel it!'

'Stop the car,' said Margo.

Joe brought the car to a stop and Margo switched on the light. 'Now,' she said briskly. 'What happened? Show me your arm.'

'There, Mammy. Above the elbow. It's all purple.'

'There's no blood,' said Margo. 'But it is red. Why did you do that, Peter?'

'I didn't touch her until she kicked me first.'

'I was asleep, Mammy. I couldn't have kicked him.'

'Mary was asleep, Peter. Why did you nip her?'

'She's a liar!' said Peter in desperation.

The sharp smack of Margo's hand across his cheek startled them all. 'How dare you!' Margo cried. 'You know very well I do not allow you to use that word. It's a horrible thing to say about your sister! I've told you over and over again – it's a word I won't allow. I just won't have it!' She looked quickly at Joe and turned away again. 'Never let me hear you use that word again! Never!'

She had to shout her last remarks to make herself heard above the noise of Peter's howling. The crying stopped his breath and he spluttered and choked with his face pressed against the upholstery of the seat. Mary sat timidly in her corner. Margo, uncertain what to do next, turned around facing the windscreen.

'There, now. There, there, there, son,' Joe began. 'You're all right.'

'I – I – I –' Peter stammered, breathing in.

'I know, I know, son. It's all right now. It's all over.'

He tried to catch Margo's eyes for permission to lean over and console the child. Her reluctance to look at him was sufficient. He stretched across the seat and lifted the shuddering boy in his arms and placed him gently on his knees. 'Now,' he said softly. 'That's better, isn't it? Much better. It's a good thing for a man to cry like that sometimes.'

The crying stopped but the light body still shook when a sob took it.

'You go to sleep there on my knee and before you know it we'll be home again. OK?' He switched off the light and started up the engine. The child was warm against his body. Soon the boy slept.

Silence filled the car. Through the mesmerism of motor, flee-ing hedges, shadows flying from the headlights, three words swam into Joe's head. 'Donging the tower.' What did Peter mean, he wondered dreamily; what game was he playing, dong-ing the tower? He recalled the child's face, engrossed, earnest with happiness, as he squatted on the ground by the rabbit hole. A made-up game, Joe supposed, already forgotten. He would ask him in the morning but Peter would not know. Just out of curiosity he would ask him, not that it mattered – And then a flutter of excitement stirred in him. Yes, yes, it did matter. Not the words, not the game, but the fact that he had seen his son, on the first good day of summer, busily, intently happy in solitude, donging the tower. The fact that Peter would never remember it was of no importance; it was his own possession now, his own happiness, this knowledge of a child's private joy.

Then, as he turned the car into the road that led to their house, a strange, extravagant thought struck him. He must have had moments of his own like Peter's, alone, back in Corradinna, donging his own towers. And, just as surely, his own father must have stumbled on him, and must have recognized himself in his son. And his father before that, and his father before that. Gen-erations of fathers stretching back and back, all finding magic and sustenance in the brief, quickly destroyed happiness of their children. The past did have meaning. It was neither reality nor dreams, neither today's patchy oaks nor the great woods of his boyhood. It was simply continuance, life repeating itself and surviving.

The Saucer of Larks

They drove the first ten miles in silence. Once, at a point where the main road veered inland and they followed a narrower track that ran along the rim of the Atlantic, the Sergeant took his pipe from between his teeth and said, 'This is all my kingdom as far as you can see,' and Herr Grass said 'Yes?' in such a way that the Sergeant was not sure if the German had understood him. He had replied 'Yes?' to so many things that the Sergeant had said that morning – questions about the work they were on and other parts of the country they had still to visit – that the old policeman resolved once more that he would keep quiet and enjoy the sun. It pleased him that the two in the rear seat, Guard Burke, his assistant, and the other German, Herr Henreich, also found conversation too difficult.

The Sergeant was a Cavan man and a garrulous man. He had been twenty-six years in Donegal but there were times when its beauty still shocked him; as on this spring morning with the sea spreading out and away into the warm sky and a high, fresh sun taking winking lights out of the granite-covered countryside. He just had to comment on it.

'Dammit, it's lovely, isn't it, eh? God Himself above you and the best of creation all round you. D'you know, only that the missus is buried away down in the midlands I wouldn't mind being laid to rest anywhere along the coast here myself.'

'Yes?' said Herr Grass. He was young and clean and polite.

'Not that it matters a curse, I suppose, where they put you when the time comes. But it would be nice to have the sea near you and the birds above you, wouldn't it?' He stole a glance at the German's face. 'And you wouldn't be disturbed every ten minutes with funerals crawling past you – I seen them myself years ago when I was stationed in Dublin. Every ten minutes they come; everyone looking sad and miserable. I'm telling you: everything's dead in them places. Once they put you in them big cemeteries you're finished all right.'

'Very depressing indeed, Sergeant,' said Guard Burke from behind, hoping to match his Sergeant's mood.

'But do you see what I mean about being buried out here in the wilds?' The Sergeant was warming up. 'Out here, it's not the same at all, Burke. Out here, man, you still have life all around you. Dammit, there's so much good life around you, you haven't a chance to be really dead!'

'Very pretty. Very pretty,' said Herr Grass.

'A grand spot,' echoed Burke.

The Sergeant, who was not too sure that he had made himself clear, stuck his pipe between his teeth again.

The car went cautiously because the surface of the road was bad. Houses became fewer. Small quilts of farms lost heart in their struggle against obdurate, peaty, rocky earth and disappeared altogether. Then there was nothing but barren bogland and here and there an occasional gnarled tree, its back to the ocean, its tortuous arms outstretched to the shelter of the interior. A long, thin promontory of about three miles in length shot out at right angles to the coastline.

'That's where we're heading,' said the Sergeant. 'Out to the tip of yon neck. That's where your man's buried. Turn right when we come to the white rock below.'

'The road – ?' began Herr Grass.

'Who would want a road out to a place like that?' said the Sergeant. 'There's a sort of a track, as far as I remember. Drive on, man!'

They drove out along the narrow strip as far as they could but half way the track became potted with rabbit holes. Herr Grass stopped suddenly.

'It is safer and quicker to walk, perhaps,' he said.

'Whatever you say,' said the Sergeant. 'A bit of a walk will take some of the mutton from beneath this shirt of mine.'

'Yes?' said Herr Grass.

'Just a manner of talking,' mumbled the Sergeant.

Herr Henreich, who had not spoken up to this, said something in German to Herr Grass and Herr Grass gave him the keys of the car. He then went back to the boot, opened it and took out a spade and a large white canvas bag which he folded neatly and placed under his arm. Herr Grass joined him and they talked rapidly together.

'Can I give you a hand there?' called the Sergeant.

'Yes?' said Herr Grass.

'Christ!' said the Sergeant softly to himself; then to Guard Burke, 'Come on, man, we'll lead the way.'

They followed the track which ran up the middle of the lean peninsula. At times it broadened into a road, wide enough to carry a car and then it would unexpectedly taper into a thin path and vanish into a bunker of sand.

'The man that battered out this route must never have sobered,' panted the Sergeant.

Burke was glad of the opening.

'What do you make of them?' he whispered confidentially.

'Make of what?'

'Them German fellas.'

'What do you mean, what do I make of them? They're doing a job of work here, a duty, just as they're doing the same duty all round the country. And we're here to see that everything's carried out legally and properly. That's what I make of them.' And, to show Burke that he was not to be drawn into any narrow criticism of the foreigners, he turned round and shouted back to the men behind, 'Do you see the wee specks in the water away south there below the island? That's the men from Gola Island shooting their lobster pots. The lobsters are exported to France and to Switzerland and to England – aye, and to your own country too. So when you go home you can say that you seen where they come from.'

'Yes?' called Herr Grass against the wind.

'What did he say?' asked the Sergeant.

' "Yes?" ' mimicked Burke accurately.

'I'm beginning to think he says that just to annoy me,' said the Sergeant.

Half a mile from the end of the promontory the path dipped sharply into a miniature valley, a saucer of green grass bordered by yellow sand dunes and the promontory itself ended in a high, blunt hill which broke the Atlantic wind. For a few seconds after they entered the valley their ears still heard the rush of the breeze and they were still inclined to call to one another. Then they became aware of the silence and then, no sooner were they hushed by it than they heard the larks, not a couple or a dozen or a score but hundreds of them, all invisible against the blue heat of the sky, an umbrella of music over this tiny world below.

'God, isn't it grand, eh?' said the Sergeant. He dropped clumsily on the grass and screwed his face up in an effort to see the birds against the light. Guard Burke sat beside him and opened the collar of his tunic. Herr Grass and Herr Henreich stood waiting. 'Dammit, could you believe that there are places like this still in the world, eh? D'you know, there are men who would give fortunes for a place like this. Fortunes. And what would they do if they got it? What would they do?'

'What, Sergeant?' asked Burke dutifully.

'They would destroy it! That's what they would do! Dig it up and flatten it out and build houses on it and ring it round with cement. Kill it. That's what they would do. Kill it. Didn't I see them myself when I was stationed in Dublin years ago, making an arse of places like Malahide and Skerries and Bray. That's what I mean. Kill it! Slaughter it!'

Herr Grass had a notebook and pencil in his hand.

'This is Glennafushog?'

'*Gleann-na-fuiseóg*', said the Sergeant, pronouncing the Gaelic name properly. 'It means "the valley of the larks". You need to be careful where you walk here: you might stand on a nest and crush it. Listen to them, man! Listen to them!' He tilted his head sideways and his mouth dropped open and his big, fleshy chest rose and fell silently. Grass and Henreich and Burke looked around them casually. After a few minutes he gathered himself together and when he spoke he avoided Grass's face.

'Herr Grass,' he began, 'I suppose you never done an irregular thing in your life?'

'Yes?'

'What I mean is' – the old policeman sought earnestly for the right words – 'I suppose you never did a wrong thing – did something that was against orders?'

'Disobey?'

The Sergeant did not like the word. He hesitated before accepting it. 'Aye – aye – disobey – that will do. Disobey. Did you ever disobey your superiors, Herr Grass?'

The German considered the question seriously. 'No –' he replied slowly. Then with finality. 'No.'

Burke was watching his Sergeant keenly.

'Neither did I neither,' said the Sergeant. 'Never. But there are times, I think, when it might not be such a bad thing to – to –' He saw Burke watching him and he looked away. 'There are times when a man could overlook orders – forget about them.'

'Overlook?' said Herr Grass.

The Sergeant got to his feet and faced the German.

'I'm going to ask you to do something.' His breath came in short puffs and he spoke quickly. 'Leave that young lad here. Don't dig him up.'

Herr Grass stiffened.

'Let him lie here where he has all that's good in God's earth around about him. He has been here for the past eighteen years; he's part of the place by now. Leave him in it. Let him rest in peace.'

'My orders are –'

'Who's to know, I ask you? Who's to tell what happened? I'll fill up whatever forms you have from your government and Burke here will cause no trouble. It will be a private thing between the four of us. No one will be a bit the wiser.'

'It is getting late. We must return to Dublin today,' said Herr Grass.

'You don't understand me,' said the Sergeant. 'I'm asking you not to touch this grave – this one. Do you understand that?' He raised his voice and said each word deliberately: 'Do not touch this grave. I will not tell anyone. Burke here will not tell. I will sign your papers.' He wheeled to his assistant. 'Burke, you try him. He doesn't understand me: it's the way I talk.'

'I understand,' said Herr Grass. 'But I have orders to obey.'

The four men stood awkwardly, looking at one another. The Sergeant's face, which had been animated and tense while he was pleading, held its concentration until the flush of anger at Grass's refusal drained out of it. Then it went flabby and a nerve under his right eye twitched spasmodically. In the silence that followed the heat of the sun poured down on them in waves. The air was a great void of warmth around them. Gradually the emptiness was filled again by the larks, slowly at first, then more and more of them until the saucer-valley shimmered with their singing.

The Sergeant's weighty body sagged in his uniform. He looked across the valley at the blunt hill.

'He was a young airman from Hamburg.' He spoke limply. 'And he crashed into that stump of a hill over there. It was a night in the summer of '42 and his plane was burned to ashes.'

Herr Grass consulted his notebook.

'First Sergeant Werner Endler,' he read.

'He was dead when I got here. And buried. The fishermen found him about fifty yards from the plane. They made a grave and laid him to rest in it before priest or anyone came because it was weather like this and the lad was badly burned.' He rubbed his hands down the legs of his trousers to dry the sweat off them.

'The exact position? Is it marked?'

'I know where it is,' said the Sergeant. 'Come on.'

He launched himself forward into the mass of heat and left the others to follow him.

The grave, a mound of grass sprinkled with wild May flowers, lay at the foot of the blunt hill. Herr Henreich opened it and put what remains he found into the white canvas bag. Then he closed the grave again and smoothed over the clay with his hands, leaving the place tidier than he had found it. While the exhumation was being done the Sergeant paced up and down a few feet from where the Germans were working and Burke went over the dunes to relieve himself. The whole job was completed within twenty minutes.

'I think that is everything,' said Herr Grass. 'Now we are prepared.'

'Right,' said the Sergeant irritably. 'We'll go, then. This bloody place is like an oven. My shirt's sticking to my back.'

On the journey back Herr Grass was more talkative. In slow, cautious English, he told them of his early childhood, of his work in the navy during the war, of his present job with the German War Graves Commission. The following day, he said, he and Herr Henreich would motor to County Clare and on the day after that to County Galway. Then they would bring all the remains to the special cemetery in County Wicklow where there were already over fifty Germans buried. Then back to Berlin where Greta and his family of three boys were waiting for him. He showed them a photograph of Greta, a plump, carefree girl in shorts, by a lake.

Back in the police station the Sergeant signed the papers which stated that he had witnessed the exhumation, and Burke signed as witness to the Sergeant's signature. Then Herr Grass and Herr Henreich added their names and left a duplicate copy of the papers with the Sergeant. They would not stay for a meal: they had to get back to Dublin that night. They thanked the two policemen for their assistance, apologized for taking up so much of their time and departed.

'They're gone,' said Burke, looking after the car.

'Aye,' said the Sergeant.

'It's no wonder they're a powerful nation; that's what I say. Did you ever see the beat of them for efficiency? And there they are away off with a dead man in the car with them and them as happy as lambs. What do you make of them, Sergeant? And did you see that second fella, the Herr Henry bucko, did you see him digging away there as if he was digging potatoes for the dinner? Never turned a hair on his head.'

'Aye.'

'And the other lad ticking off the names in his wee book like a grocer. Aw, but they're a powerful race of people. Powerful. And then when –'

'Aye, powerful,' echoed the Sergeant, not knowing what he was saying. Then straightening his shoulders and pushing his stomach in with the flat of his hand, he said briskly, 'Now, Burke, back inside with us to our own duties. Have you distributed those handbills about the dog licences?'

'This afternoon, Sergeant, I was going to do it.'

'And the tillage census in the upper parish, have you finished it yet?'

'All but three or four houses, Sergeant. I'll do them in a while of an evening on the bicycle.'

'Good,' said the Sergeant. 'That'll be that, then.' The moment of efficiency died in him as quickly as it had begun. His shoulders slumped and his stomach crept out. 'I don't know a damn what came over me out there,' he said in a low voice, as if he were alone.

'What's that, Sergeant?'

'What in hell came over me? I never did the like of it in my life before. Never in all my years in the force. And then before foreigners too.' He raised his cap inches above his head, slipped his fingers under it and fumbled with his scalp. He lowered the cap again. 'I'm damned if I can understand it. The heat, maybe. The heat and the years – they're a treacherous combination, Burke, very treacherous.'

'What are you talking about, Sergeant?' said Burke with exaggerated innocence.

'You know bloody well what I'm talking about. And I'll tell you something here and now, Burke.' He prodded the guard's shoulder with his index finger. 'If ever a word of what happened out there at Glennafushog breaks your lips, to any mortal man, now or ever, as God's my judge, Burke, I'll have you sent to the wildest outpost in the country. Now, get away out with you and distribute them handbills.'

'Very good, Sergeant.'

'And report to me again when you come back.'

'Righto, Sergeant. Righto.'

The Sergeant turned and waddled towards the building. For a man of his years and shape he carried himself with considerable dignity.

Everything Neat and Tidy

The County Psychiatric Clinic, situated a discreet three miles beyond the town boundary, was made up of two distinct groups of buildings, as contrasting as two figures in a parable. There was the old block, originally the Mental Hospital, a granite fortress with lean, high windows and black iron doors, where the 'permanently unwell' now crooned or sobbed or fluttered away their remaining days. One hundred and fifty yards away, at the end of a dividing patch that was neither field nor lawn, there was the new block, the pride of the County Health Authority – a collection of pastel-coloured chalets with large glass doors and windows where 'temporarily disturbed' people made model aeroplanes or lampshades or raffia mats with eager, brittle concentration. It was to the new block that Johnny Barr drove Mrs MacMenamin, his mother-in-law, in his taxi every Tuesday and Thursday morning during the whole of the month of March.

At the time of Mr Mac's death and, indeed, for three weeks afterwards, Mrs Mac had been wonderful. The anguish and indignity that his sudden death had let loose – the invasion by the bailiffs, the indecent haste with which the bank sold the house and the farm off to the first bidder, the shooting of the two obese, useless Labradors (who wanted two gun-shy gun dogs?), getting Sarah, the old housekeeper, accepted in the Old People's Home run by the Nazareth nuns, and only after much pleading – all this she had borne so quietly and so courageously that Johnny realized he had never known her before. Previously, he had thought of her as a vague, diffident, impractical woman. Now he admired her. So that when her son, Henry, who was a doctor, ignored her requests to go and live with him in his flat in Dublin Johnny promptly offered her the spare room in his neat terraced house with his wife, Mary, and himself. She accepted and he was glad to have her. It never occurred to him that this would strike her as the final, crushing indignity.

For three weeks she behaved as if nothing in her life had changed. She read in her bedroom, or did a little light house-work, or sometimes just sat in the tiny, precise parlour and gazed out placidly at the children playing in the street after school. Then, one Sunday after supper, when Johnny and Mary were worrying over the problem of whether they should go ahead and buy a second taxi, Mrs MacMenamin began to cry quietly. Johnny was the first to notice her tears.

'It's OK, Mrs Mac,' he said. He winked at her. 'Even if a second cab leaves us short for a while we won't put you out to work!'

Before he had finished speaking she began to moan. Her moaning grew into a wail, and the wail thinned and rose to a shriek, and when they held her, Johnny by the right arm and Mary by the left, she flung back her head and screamed and screamed at the ceiling. The paroxysm lasted less than a minute. When her struggling was strongest and her distraught cries broke against the walls of the confining room she suddenly went limp. They carried her long, awkward body upstairs and laid her on the bed, and tiptoed down again and talked in whispers. Later, the doctor called and said, 'Reaction – nerves – temporary –' and arranged for an appointment for her at the County Psychiatric Clinic. The clinic advised electric-shock treatments – two times a week, nine treatments in all – and Johnny took on the job of driving her there and back because there was no one else to do it and because ever since that Sunday night, seeing her so helpless and so pale and so exposed on top of the bedclothes, his admiration for her had turned into affection.

Johnny came to enjoy those trips to the clinic. Occasionally he calculated that they were costing him a lot of money (in wear and tear on the car, not to talk of lost fares), but it was pleasant to get away from the smelly taxi rank and out into the keen spring air of the country. While he waited for Mrs Mac he walked around the grounds admiring the trim paths and the careful gardens and the tidy shrubs and thinking how lucky he was – a wife who loved and respected him (and who had now become so thrifty that her watchfulness sometimes annoyed him), a compact, comfortable home, a business that was expanding. Every morning, too, he stood and gazed for a short time across the patch of land that was neither field nor lawn and then, for some reason, his thoughts invariably went back to the time before he was married, when he went out to the MacMenamins' farm every Sunday afternoon to take Mary for a drive. But most of the waiting time he spent strolling around the chalets which, to all outward appearances, might have been a collection of summer holiday houses.

After four or five visits Johnny was convinced that the electric-shock treatments were a failure. The only effect they had on Mrs Mac – and he did not mention this to Mary because it lasted for only about twenty minutes after the old woman came out of the sky-blue chalet – was to make her arrogant and overbearing, even more imperious than Lady Hartnell of Killard whom he drove to the bank once a month. Mrs Mac would march up to the taxi and climb into the back seat and say, 'Off you go, John!' as if he were her private chauffeur. Of course the treatments temporarily impaired her memory – the doctor had told him to expect that – and as he drove her home he protected himself against her bumptiousness by encouraging her confusion. It was harmless enough fun, Johnny asking her how things were on the farm these days and she replying that Mr Mac had just bought a huge combine harvester, or the latest milking machine, or a very expensive pedigree bull. Or Johnny would wonder out loud how the spring sowing was going and she would list off such a series of crops as the biggest farm in the whole of Ireland could never have produced. The grander she got with him the more he chuckled to himself. But by the time he drew up at the door her affectations all vanished and her memory came back and she was a silent, timid, tearful, ageing woman again. He helped her out of his taxi and guided her tenderly into the house and handed her over to his wife as gently as if she were a baby because then, seeing her so reduced, and remembering her as she had once been, he regretted his baiting and resolved never to mention the farm again.

The MacMenamins never had the wealth or the position of Lady Hartnell of Killard. But they might have had Mr Mac not drunk so heavily, had Mrs Mac been more practical, had they kept Henry on the farm (and it was one of the best farms in County Tyrone) instead of making a doctor of him, had the rich land been worked and not let to neighbours. They lived imprudently, carelessly, without thought for the future. When he recalled those Sunday afternoons Johnny remembered the feeling of annoyance that had pricked him every time he saw electric lights burning all over the house in broad daylight, the apples rotting in barrels in the pantry, the wrought-iron gates hanging from one hinge, or the buckets rusting in the water troughs. Every time he went there he wanted to throw off his coat and fix fences, paint doors, and gather up fallen branches for firewood. So much waste. Such great indifference. He would knock at the door; no one would answer, and he would go into the high, panelled hall. Mr Mac would be in a deep sleep before a dead fire in the drawing room, or puzzling futilely over pages of figures and accounts. Mrs Mac would be upstairs, reading in one of the bedrooms, or crocheting in the breakfast room. Sarah, the old housekeeper, would be dozing in the kitchen, although the table would be piled high with the lunch dishes. Even Mary, who knew to expect him, was seldom waiting for him. He would find her in the fields wandering around in search of hens' nests or down in one of the byres playing with a litter of young pups.

The whole set-up confused and annoyed him and yet fascinated him. When he was with them he was conscious only of importance. What a business he would have made of that place! How he could have run it! Yet when he went home to his own house in the town – before he married he lived in three rooms as natty and precise as a doll's house, above the bakery where his father was nightwatchman – he forgot the chaos and the decay and remembered only the tranquillity of their lives. He would look at his mother, birdlike, shrivelled, sharp with the lifelong battle against poverty, and think of Mrs Mac who had floated serenely above hardships. He would watch his father roll cigarettes (by making his own, he saved threepence a packet) and remember the carpet at Mrs Mac's feet ruined by cigar burns. The contrast between the life he had been reared to and the life he now tasted made him dissatisfied with both. It would have taken so little, he knew, to win him over to the MacMenamins. If Mr Mac had said even once to him, 'You're early today,' or 'We thought you were never coming,' or if Mrs Mac had asked him even once what his job was or what his ambitions were, then there would have been no conflict. But they gave him as little of their attention as they gave to one another, or to the land, or to the fat, wheezing Labradors which wandered unheeded upstairs and downstairs. And still, those Sunday-afternoon visits were the highlight of his week. It was not for Mary alone that he spread his trousers under the mattress every Saturday night so that they would have a sharp crease, and bathed himself in the iron tub in the miniature scullery, and polished his shoes until they glistened. It was primarily for her, of course; but it was also for Mrs Mac, and even for Mr Mac, and, in some vague way that he could not understand himself, out of deference to the ramshackle farm itself.

In the last week of Mrs Mac's course of treatments Mary came across the notice of Sarah's death in the Home. Johnny agreed that the news must be kept from Mrs Mac. If she was making progress – and there was little evidence that she was – this would set her back. Yet – when she came out of the clinic later that morning and said to him, 'Hurry up! I have shopping to do! Don't sit there leering at me!' – he knew he was going to tell her.

He waited until they had passed through the gates. Then he said, 'How do you feel today, Mrs Mac?'

'Quite well, thank you, John.' She looked very alert that day, much better than after any of the previous treatments.

'One more visit and you're finished up, Mrs Mac.'

'I know.'

'What will you do with yourself then?'

'I haven't decided yet. Travel, maybe. Go to London for a few weeks. D'you know, I haven't been in London since Henry qualified.' Her eyes became troubled. 'But travel is so expensive, isn't it?' she went on. 'It takes so much money, doesn't it?'

'As well as that you couldn't very well leave the farm at this time of year,' he prompted.

'Yes,' she said, but so dreamily that he knew she was agreeing with her own private thoughts.

'This is your busiest time on the land, isn't it, Mrs Mac? This is the time all you farmers work a sixteen-hour day, isn't it?'

'Yes,' she said in the same vague way. 'Quite right – yes –'

He watched her in the mirror to see the brows furrow in concentration and the lips fumble with one another as they always did on these trips home. But not today. There was going to be no harmless fun today. An uneasiness stirred in him. 'I suppose you heard about Sarah, Mrs Mac?'

'Sarah? Who's Sarah?'

'Sarah, the old housekeeper. You remember Sarah, don't you? Always giving backchat to you!'

'I – yes, I think I remember her.'

'I knew you would.'

He paused, conscious of cruelty. But before he could muster charity he heard himself saying, 'She died last night.'

'Sarah? My housekeeper?'

'Funeral tomorrow after last Mass.'

'Sarah?' she whispered.

'Dead,' he said.

'Ooh, God!' She did not cry, but she moaned. She gripped her elbows and rocked herself backwards and forwards and groaned in a high monotone that terrified him. He thought of stopping the taxi, of getting her a drink of brandy, of rushing her to a doctor, but then decided instead to get her home as quickly as possible.

By the time they reached the house she had quietened. He put his arm around her and supported her into the hallway where Mary met them.

'Quick!' he snapped. 'Get her bed ready!'

Mary stared stupidly at them.

'For God's sake, move!' he roared, because he was afraid that Mrs Mac would collapse in his arms. 'Move! Move! Move!'

He lifted her off the ground – she was as light as a child – and carried her upstairs as tenderly and as lovingly as if she were a baby. Afterwards, when she was asleep and he was having a meal, Mary kissed him on the forehead and said, 'Thank you, Johnny. You've been better to her than any son could have been.' He did not answer because he was angry with himself, because he felt guilty, and because he was frightened. There had been a moment in the taxi, after Mrs Mac did not respond to his first prompting about the farm, when a strange loneliness had touched him; what frightened him was that that loneliness, that isolation, might touch him again, might even enter into him.

The following Thursday was Mrs Mac's last visit. It was a glorious spring morning that was both urgent and still. The sun was high, and the air was clean and clear, and the grounds had never looked fresher nor more attractive. He walked round the paths and looked at the flowers he had seen push into life, and strolled between the neat, trimmed shrubs. It was a morning for alertness, a morning when a man can look back over the past and take pride in his achievements, and look forward to the future and plan confidently for it. But somehow Johnny was conscious only of wistfulness. There was growth and vitality around him and beneath him but his senses were muted with a vague nostalgia. He left the new block and gazed across the patch that was neither field nor lawn. And then, for the first time, he understood the clinic's special attraction for him. It could have been a part of the farm. This discovery, and the start of recognition that accompanied it, gave him a moment's pleasure, a delight that vanished as soon as it was felt. It gave way to a quick, flooding panic. To hell with the farm, he thought, angrily marching back to the new block! To hell with it! To hell with it!

Mrs Mac found him in the waiting room, reading magazines. He jumped to his feet when he saw her.

'All set?' he said.

'At long last. Let's get home quickly, Johnny. I never want to see this place again.' And she giggled nervously because she thought that a nurse who was passing might have heard her.

They got into the taxi. For the first time she sat beside him in the front. He waited for 'Off you go, John!' but it did not come. As they passed through the gates he took a quick look back at the grounds and the two groups of buildings. They looked chaste and festive in the sunlight.

Mrs Mac smiled happily at the road ahead. 'Someday, Johnny, I'll have to repay you for all these trips. You have been more than kind to me.'

'There's only one way you can repay me, Mrs Mac,' he said, laughing unnaturally.

'What way is that?'

'Leave me the farm when you die.'

'There's no one deserves it more,' she said.

Johnny remained silent, frowning to himself. Mrs Mac seemed much better today; she was almost complacent. For some reason he did not understand each improvement in her health seemed to add to a growing melancholy inside himself. Now he tried to take heart from the ambiguity of her last reply. So she really thought she still owned the farm, did she?

'Is this – is this Wednesday, Johnny?' Mrs Mac said.

'Thursday,' he said.

'Then I'm a day late.'

'Late for what, Mrs Mac?'

'For the funeral – Sarah's funeral.'

'Sarah was buried a week ago, Mrs Mac. You're not a day late – you're eight days late!'

'Eight days? How – where – where did the time go?'

'How should I know?' he snapped. Then, persuasively, he added, 'I was at the funeral.'

'Oh, you were? That's good. I'm glad we were represented.'

'No one there but myself. The only mourner.'

'Poor Sarah,' she said, dismissing her with a sigh. 'May God have mercy on her.'

'Remember how she used to sleep in front of the fire, Mrs Mac? Remember? She would pile up the dishes and pull up a comfortable chair and spread herself out and –'

'She was so stupid,' said Mrs Mac briskly. 'At least half a dozen times I taught her how to make pastry. But she never could learn. She really was a peasant, Sarah.'

'Pastry?' he said, pouncing on the scrap of new information.

'And so lazy! Heavens, how I stood her for so long! But let's think of pleasant things, shall we? D'you know, Johnny, it'll be summer before we know it.' She smiled serenely out at the countryside. 'I wonder what Mary'll have for lunch today,' she said interestedly.

Mary was waiting for them at the door, dancing with

excitement; Henry was coming from Dublin that evening to take Mrs Mac back with him. There had been a letter in the midday delivery, and on its heels a telegram with the same news. He had forgotten he had written! So typical of Henry!

Mrs Mac took the news as calmly as if she had expected it. 'Henry was always a good boy,' she said to Mary. 'But I love your Johnny every bit as dearly now. He has been as good to me as any son.' She went upstairs to pack.

Johnny pretended that he had a run to do. He dashed out of his house, sprang into his taxi, and drove recklessly towards the centre of the town. He steered wildly, in full stampede, and through the windscreen he saw only the farm as he had known it in all its autumn decay and beauty. Mrs Mac had escaped. She was at peace, no longer frightened by the past and the morass of memory, but her release had deprived him forever of the farm and the Sunday afternoons and all the tidy, attainable ambitions of his single days. Chilled by this sudden personal disaster he drove faster and faster, as if he could escape the moment when he would take up the lonely burden of recollections that the dead had fled from and the living had forgotten.